A COWBOY CHRISTMAS

AN AMERICAN TALE

Praise for *A Cowboy Christmas An American Tale*

"It's good and it moves! Tom Van Dyke tells a rousing tale of a young man learning how to cowboy and finding the girl of his dreams. I've written a good 40 western stories but learned a lot from Tom's book."

—ELMORE LEONARD
Novelist

"INSPIRING. *A Cowboy Christmas An American Tale* reveals the true American West but goes even further. A man and woman who refuse to let a soaring relationship disappear is a sign of life on earth at its best."

—MICHAEL BLAKE
Author of *Dances With Wolves*

"A Cowboy Christmas is a wonderful tale of a young cowboy's roam and a heartfelt love story. A great Christmas story and a delightful read for all seasons."

—THOMAS COBB
Author of *Crazy Heart*

"I'm a narrative painter, so as I read this book, the words drew pictures in my mind. These images are vivid and the story feels real. *A Cowboy Christmas An American Tale*, is a welcome addition to my library."

—HOWARD TERPNING
Western Artist

"A GREAT RIDE!"

"*A Cowboy Christmas* is a warm, well-written tale of a young man discovering himself and the new world during an engaging adventure in the American West. I thoroughly enjoyed the picture painted by the words of Mr. Van Dyke. The book took me back in time and sparked memories of when I was working on Western films with my friend John Wayne."

"*A Cowboy Christmas An American Tale* is a beautiful story for all ages. Not since the work of James Dickey have I read such poetry in a novel. A wonderful remembrance for what the Old West once was. Don't wait for the film—buy the book now."

"Tom Van Dyke has crafted an inspired story of the Old West, Arizona and New Mexico Territories—1873. A well-researched tale of an adventuresome young man, carving out a life that most men can only dream about. Hold on tight. It's a fast ride. This magical tale fits like a vintage Stetson and good pair of boots."

A COWBOY CHRISTMAS

AN AMERICAN TALE

To Alex

keep Writing

TOM VAN DYKE

T V Dyke

PAGE BRANCH PUBLISHING
PHOENIX, ARIZONA

Third Revised Edition 2012 with additions and matter of fact

Copyright © 2009, 2010, 2012 Tom Van Dyke. All rights reserved.
Page Branch Publishing, Phoenix, Arizona

A Cowboy Christmas An American Tale

is a work of historical fiction. Names, characters and events are

products of the author's imagination. All characters, events and any

resemblance to persons, living or dead is coincidental.

ISBN: 978-0-615-31837-0

Manufactured in the United States of America

5 7 9 8 6 4

Elizabeth Wideman, Editor
Ellen Alsever, Editor

Mary Van Dyke, Book Design

Douglas Carn, Text

Bob Coronato, Cover Art
Original Chine Colle' Etching
"High Roller"

Please Support Our Libraries, Museums and National Parks

Visit: ACowboyChristmas.com
for Special Features and Particulars.

For

Mary, who has inspired and shared every trail

And

Adam, Mark, Grant, Jocelyn and Walker

who made it a joy

PREFACE

I have a long trail of praise for the American cowboy.

Leafing through tattered pages of hand-written journals and dust-covered books, and wandering museums admiring masterworks of western artists, I looked beyond the golden frames as windows into America's past and imagined what the restless spirit of the West was like one hundred fifty years ago for cowboys on the American frontier.

Inspired, I felt challenged to create a magical story that crisscrosses the expansion of the far West and collides with destiny—a story about cowboys who burned themselves like candles for experiences worth living and values that created strength and revealed character—a story as enduring as the romance of the West.

Embracing a cowboy's flavorful soup of words and expressions, WB tells his story with cowboy wit and humor. His tale begins in 1873. Not yet sixteen, with hope and dreams, he crosses the Mississippi and without fear leaves the far shore of civilization behind. With empty pockets, a spark for life, and a wild sense of freedom, he follows his heart searching for adventure and fortune and discovers the romance.

"Columbus discovered America in 1492
Horses arrived in 1519
Cattle arrived in 1521
Then there were C o w b o y s"

—tom van dyke

CONTENTS

A COWBOY CHRISTMAS

AN AMERICAN TALE

Christmas Eve 1908

WHITE BILLOWING CLOUDS drift across the endless blue sky, floating over the open range for as far as the eye can see. Only the majesty of the snow-capped mountain peaks could grace the pristine beauty and tranquility of the western frontier.

The faint sound of galloping hooves becomes louder, louder, louder and explodes with a herd of cattle stampeding up and over the rise chased by Model T automobiles driven by cowboys.

The spring roundup is a circus with fifteen cowboys yipping and hollering while driving Model Ts racing along and circling the thundering herd of twenty-five hundred head.

Young, handsome and wild, these cowboys wheel the Model Ts, bumping and grinding, weaving around and zipping up alongside the herd trying to swing the leaders. Dust from the cattle covers their windshields. One of the cowboy drivers is wearing a broad-brimmed, high-crown Stetson. Glass driving goggles cover his eyes and a neckerchief is pulled up over his nose and tied around his face to protect him from the dust. Banging on the door with his hand, "Yip! Yip! Yip!" he races in close alongside the leaders. All the Model T cowboys are darting about maneuvering around for position and trying to gain control of the raging herd.

The barking of a dog interrupts the cowboys of this fantasy roundup. WB, cowboy handsome, is playing a harmonica and fanning his vintage Stetson, yahooing around the evening campfire. It is a chilly Christmas Eve and he is wearing a faded wool cardigan with leather buttons.

He pushes back his silver hair, brushes tears of laughter from his weathered eyes and fingers his mustache. His dog is jumping up on his leg excitedly barking at him. "OK, Beans. You can come along."

Back in his fantasy herding cattle, WB is driving one of the Model Ts. Beans is jumping around on the seat next to him watching the cattle as they run alongside.

Racing across the range, leaving a trail of dust, another cowboy is hauling a bawling calf in the back seat of a Model T Ford and cuts WB off.

Jamming the gears and stomping on the brakes, WB swerves, sliding to a dusty stop.

Again, barking interrupts this Model T folly.

Dancing around by the campfire and mouthing a final flourish on the harmonica, WB laughs out loud enjoying his fantasy. Beans jumps up on a stump and continues barking at him. "OK. OK, Beans." Laughing, "Easy, easy." Looking at the steaming Dutch oven that hangs on a hook from a steel tripod, he lifts the lid and takes in a deep breath. "Delicious." Beans jumps off the stump and WB settles down by the fire.

WB picks up the wrinkled advertisement, torn from a magazine, that he had dropped in the excitement. There, in picture and print for all the world to see, is Henry Ford's Model T horseless carriage. "A horseless carriage. Imagine that." He is quite taken by the news of such an invention.

He laughs, envisioning cowboys riding horseless carriages and imagines a Henry Ford chuck wagon, driven by a Mexican cook with a large sombrero. This Model T is bowed up with a covered wagon canvas, clanking with gear and supplies, chugging and zigzagging across the range.

At lunch on the cattle drive, cowboys are rushing in, driving Model T stallions to grub a quick plate of chuck. They are surrounded by a rough string of black Model Ts with their motors sputtering and ready to roll out.

And on the range, WB pictures himself sitting comfortably in the backseat of the Model T with his legs stretched out playing his harmonica. A cowboy is driving the rig and another rides shotgun. Sitting next to WB, high on the back of the seat, a wrangler twirls a rope with a huge loop encircling the entire Model T automobile as the cowboys drift over the range.

Returning to reality, he's talking to himself, "Cowboying will be downright enjoyable." WB laughs at his vision of the Model T cowboys. He is just about to return to the adventures of his mind, when the low-rolling growl of Beans herds him back. "Alright, OK," laughing at himself. Beans sits guard at his boots.

WB turns from the fire and lectures, "Beans, this fire tells no lies; it burns hot, sparks the imagination, needs constant tending and in smoke drifts away." Pointing at Beans, "Now you remember that." Beans curls his tongue in a deep yawn.

Staring back at the advertisement for Henry Ford's Model T automobile, WB realizes, like the smoke of the fire, he has drifted into another age.

The smell of the mesquite fire fills the air as smoke curls up from the chimney of the old adobe ranch house.

The front door opens with the sound of little bells. Stepping out, and caught between the moonlight and the warm glow of the house, his wife, Ginny, a striking woman with silver-streaked hair, says, "Sounds like a rodeo out here. What'cha two up to?"

Engaged in thought over the advertisement, WB does not hear her.

Walking over to the fire, Ginny glances at the Henry Ford Model T automobile advertisement gripped in his hands.

"For me? Ain't we gonna look grand putt-putt-puttin' uptown to buy me a new bonnet and a satin parasol."

"It won't take us but a minute to get there. Henry's Model T brand travels twenty-five miles in an hour."

"I'm driving."

"No doubt."

"Well, at least Mr. Ford got the color right."

Kissing him on the cheek, Ginny softly says, "Merry Christmas, cowboy. My present for you isn't so grand. I got you an ax and a grubbing hoe." She laughs and WB kisses her. Ginny moves over to the Dutch oven and lifts the lid. "Supper's ready."

WB says, "I'll bring it in."

"Sit tight, I got it."

Watching Ginny, he wishes her, "Merry Christmas, Darlin'. I'll be right in."

WB smiles and returns to the fire. Treasuring times past, he lingers and pictures one last memory. The year is 1876. WB is a young cowboy flying through the air fanning his hat, whirling around on the arched back of an exploding bronc mustang, whipping up the dust and punching holes in the clouds.

Smiling, he says, "Good ride, cowboy."

He stands and gathers some kindling. Stopping for a moment, he takes in a deep breath, gazing at the moonlight's reflection from the creek onto the silver cottonwoods. In a whisper he says, "A horseless carriage." Crumpling up the magazine page advertising the future, he tosses it into the flames and smiles, "I still have my fire."

The door opens and WB enters the house. Bells attached to a wreath made of vines and berries rattle as the door closes on Beans who squeezes through.

WB grouses, "Pokey Beans, there was a time you'd a tripped me up, beatin' me through that door." On his way to the hearth, WB glances at the artist easel with his painting of wild mustangs racing across a western landscape. "I hope they like it."

"They're going to love it," praises Ginny while

slicing up the roast.

"What time are those grandbabies arriving tomorrow?"

"Oh, probably start drifting in late morning."

Beans wanders over to her. Sensing his presence and with perfect timing, she lowers a trim of meat and Beans gently takes it from her hand.

"Pretty out tonight," she says.

WB ambles over and gives her a kiss. "Pretty inside tonight."

She smiles. "That's cowboy talk with romance on his mind. Why don't you light the candles?"

WB walks over to a shelf where photographs of the children and their wedding portrait hang on the wall. Pausing, he studies the pictures and then picks the candles from the shelf. "Both of them?"

Ginny smiles, "Well?"

"Well what?"

"I'm ready for romance. Tell me your Christmas story," she coaxes.

Chunking the fire he teases, "You know that story by heart."

"I know. But I like the way you whittle the tale."

Ginny has reminded WB to tell his story every Christmas Eve for as long as they've been together.

Pulling a kindling stick from the fire, he lights the candles and begins a story he likes to tell. The drama of his voice matches the landscape of his face and the gleam in his eyes. Deep, weathered and steady with an easy way, WB begins.

Blowing in the Wind

BLOWING IN THE WIND, I wasn't much more than a hayseed, fifteen years old, when I stowed away on a ship crossing the Atlantic Ocean from the old country, on the trail for adventure, discovery, and fortune in the new world. It was the year I gave up my gold and silver—1873. With the gold sovereign from my parents, I bought an Indian pony and a high-horned Mexican saddle from a trader. I traded the silver pocket watch my father had given me for an American rifle and I was off. I was looking to ripen in the far West.

Chasing the rainbow, I started my roam. I crossed the Mississippi and left the muddy bank of civilization as I knew it. Rumors of land with vast riches, and the discovery of California gold lying on the ground no deeper than a carrot, had set off a stampede of white-hooded wagons migrating in pandemonium for the land of the setting sun.

The further I plowed from civilization the more of it I found. Furniture and other items of good intention too heavy for ox or mule to haul another day were left, picked over and strewn along the trails.

And then with certain predictability, miles up ahead, I'd find graves marked with headboards and the bleached bones of an ox or horse that travelers were forced to slaughter for lack of food and planning. This was common sight.

Trail-weary mules would haul to a stand-off, refusing to budge. Negotiations began with a crack of the whip followed by a barrage of verbal encouragements blistering the ears of the mules and not fit for the lessons of Sunday school. Another household item would sail from the wagon.

Having rested for two hours and satisfied their terms had been addressed, the victors, with another crack of a whip, would launch a momentary charge of the trail. The dust would flood over the top of the wagon wheels and through the spaces between the loops of the canvas ties into the wagon.

This combined folly of tongue, temper, whip and grunt created a sight that made the covered wagons appear to float like boats on billowing waves in clouds of dust.

Between the torrid sun and the endless dust, faces burned and noses bled from the dry cutting dust which covered every man, woman and child inside and out.

Having endured the endless solitude, monotony and arid expanse of the Great Plains, I slowly approached the foothills of the Rocky Mountains.

Overcome by thirst, I was losing my song and enthusiasm for the lore of the West.

The trail was cluttered with settlers, Yankee neighbors, Rebel brothers, white marauders, men with all the earmarks of bad company—and me.

For safety and good company, I thought it best to attach myself to a wagon train.

I was breezing by when I noticed her brushing her hair in the back of the wagon. Oh my!—she was made of sugar. I slowed my pony to a walk and her wagon passed me by. Keeping up alongside with the rolling wagon, I removed my hat and said, "Hello. Allow me to introduce myself."

"Hello," she smiled.

I loved her at first sight. Ginny had long flowing golden hair, divine eyes, sculpted features and cherry lips.

We talked and laughed and in time discovered each other. Smart and witty, she was raised on books. Cuddling by campfires and stargazing, we studied the heavens and watched the shooting stars leave trails in the sky. "There's the Big Dipper," pointed Ginny.

"Right beside Polaris, the North Star," I said.

"And together they are the time keepers for the heavens," said Ginny. "The Big Dipper rotates counter-clockwise around the North Star every twenty-four hours." Holding her hand above her head she clinched her fist, pointing her forefinger straight up as the handle and with her thumb straight out, like the front edge of the Dipper. "The North Star is off to the right of my thumb. It's ten o'clock now and the Dipper is here." Moving her hand, "At midnight it will be here, at two a.m. it

will be here, and at four a.m., here."

Reaching over, I cupped my hands into a pail of water. "This is for you, Ginny." I held my hands out to her.

"What's for me?"

"Look." Ginny leaned in and peered at the moon's reflection in the water cupped in my hands.

". . .Oh! . . . Is this a promise?"

Gazing at Ginny in the glow of the full moon, she looked like a porcelain doll.

". . .Promise?" I asked. It was the first time a girl had ever gazed upon me with such loveliness, opening feelings of passion to me and my emotions.

"Are you promising me the Moon?"

I delighted in her gaze. Our back-and-forth volley in that tender moment was my awakening. Her glow gave my heart flight. So pure she was, I fumbled for words rising to her poetry.

"I promise you the Moon. . . and under all the stars in heaven I will love only you all the days of my life."

Her smile captured me and we held each other close for a long time when Ginny whispered, "My heart belongs to you."

We were inseparable. And, in the tall grass, we stole away. It was the happiest time of my life.

And Ginny wasn't far behind. She told her mother, "He loves me Mama and I love him."

"No you don't, Ginny! How do you know?" Concerned, "How can you tell?"

"His eyes tell me. The way they lay on me. He's strong and smart too." Ginny was passionate, "I got feelings for him Mama, his lips, his. . ."

Putting her hands to her ears, "Hush child, you froth too much."

Ginny had a natural innocence that required vigilance and for her folks to be on constant watch for coyotes.

Her father took one look at WB and knew: tall, lean and good-looking, he's on the loose.

We were rumbling around in the back of the covered wagon out of view. Ginny's mama was driving the team. Ginny was giggling and laughing when Mama yelled back, "Virginia, what's goin' on back there?"

". . .Nothin', Mama."

Well, Mama let out a whistle that could cut glass. "Virgil," she squalled, "Ginny's bundling up again."

We scampered, getting ourselves together knowing the chaperone was on his way, a big man with an Arkansas toothpick.

Lickety-split, I climbed out of the work end of the covered wagon, untied my pony that was trailing along and jumped on. By the time Pa busts up, I was a choirboy with my harmonica, serenading my prairie madonna.

He flashed around the big knife, gesturing he's going to shave me real close.

"Oh, Pa, W's just playing me a melody."

If looks could kill, I had just been wounded.

Squinting hard and drawing the toothpick under his eyes, "Walker Brady, I'm eyein' you, boy." Slowly, Pa put the big knife back into its sheath and rode back up ahead. Ginny smiled and I trotted along with my serenade.

"I don't think your pa likes my music."

Dancing With Pain

THE ARIZONA TERRITORY was opening up and we were on an ancient Indian trail used by the Apache and the Yavapai. The military out of Fort McDowell had widened the trail into a wagon road as a short cut to the West. Indian raids and attacks were random and often. We were a day out from the bubbling springs of Cave Creek where we figured the trail divided off in the direction towards Phoenix, Wickenburg and the gold fields.

Word coming back down the trail from weary travelers returning to the United States, was that just beyond Black Mountain the trail was marked by a giant hellcat cactus tree. "You can't miss it." We were warned to avoid the sharp fortress of thorny hitchhiking fruits. Their sharp barbs pierced clothing, and drew blood with penetrating pain to arms and legs.

This trail cactus had gathered tattered pieces of clothing and canvas from wagons passing too close. Travelers began leaving personal items and notes on the cactus for members of their party bringing up the rear. And that was us, three covered wagons picking up the rear. We were looking for a note telling us which trail our wagon train had chosen, and then we'd follow on.

It was late afternoon. I was poking along on my pony. The girl of my dreams, pretty as a picture in sundress and bonnet, was framed in the canvas at the rear of the covered wagon. She could hardly keep her eyes off me. Our passions were again suddenly interrupted when I noticed four Indians with rifles taking position undercover up on a knoll. They'd been dogging our lumbering wagons all morning and now they were setting up ahead to swoop down and ambush.

"Apache! Get down," I warned Ginny. I quick-kicked my pony to a gallop and rode up alongside the wagons to warn the others. "Apache! Apache! Apache!"

Up ahead on the dusty trail, the wagons were rolling around a sharp turn and the giant cactus that guarded the trail. I pulled up alongside the lead wagon just about the time it was passing the thorny, spiked sentry of the trail. The wagon jolted out of the wheel ruts, scaring my pony and I was thrown into the embrace of the messenger of pain. Captured and held in the nest of thorns, I hung there and slowly untangled falling and tumbling to the ground.

Now whether it was seeing and fearing the Indians, or just Ginny's pa's way of saying goodbye, the dusty wagons kept rolling. I fell to the ground, covered with the thorny fruits from hell.

Rolling around, jerking and spinning in terrible anguish, I looked up and saw the Indians. Distracted from their ambush, they were no longer aiming their rifles at the wagons. They were laughing at me.

Covered with the thorny fruits, I tried to remove the barbs from my flesh, but the more I struggled, the worse it got. The barbed fruit stuck in my fingers, arms and legs, through my clothes and appeared to be growing from my hat while my boots sprouted toes.

All the while, the laughing Indians watched my flailing painful dance. Lowering their rifles, they must have felt my agony. They mounted their ponies and rode off.

Lying there, the last thing I remembered was looking up and thinking that the cactus tree actually looked pretty with its golden thorns backlit by the setting sun.

Oh Lordy, it was not a silent night! I passed out into a nightmare of pain and soon encountered the devil's own flock—hairy-whiskered critters with a terrible stench. They sniffed, snorted and dribbled feasting on the buffet of cactus fruits. I was their banquet table. All night they roamed until they started nibbling at my toes.

Startled, I woke up. The black musk hogs of my dreams were eating the thorny fruits from my boots. They had plucked and eaten near every one from my body. As I rose up, they snorted and scampered off. Praise the Lord.

My pony stayed faithful and grazed nearby. I

got up slowly dusting myself off looking for thorns. Resting there in the cuff of my trousers, I spied a pearl button on a thread.

I looked over the giant cactus for a note. There was none. Carefully, I removed the few barbed fruits from my saddle blanket and crawled onto my pony.

I found the trail marker with wood arrows pointing the way to: Phoenix, Wickenburg, Gold Fields and Indians. Looking over the crossroad, I tried to read which trail the wagons traveled and carried my true love away. With visions of fortunes to be made, the trails to both the gold fields and Wickenburg were well tracked, leaving no clue to which route Ginny's wagon traveled.

Slowly regaining full possession of my mind, I placed full blame for my misfortune squarely where it belonged, "Bonehead!" My pony's ears perked straight up and he began to dance around. "What were you thinking? Did you see what happened to me back there? Ginny's gone! . . . Which way did they go?" He settled and wisely looked over the trails from right to left. "And don't be repeating another Oklahoma on me." Giving him his head, he chose the trail to the gold fields.

Boy, was he wrong.

Dust to Dust

MY TRUE LOVE had vanished. I found myself alone. Down and out, I took grunt work in the gold fields looking for pay dirt alongside the Chinamen. The grip of gold fever had every poor man believing that every shovel, every pan and every blast would be the next mother lode, only to be left with empty pockets, shattered dreams and a broken heart.

Washing gold from placer gravel was hard, unproductive work. Cleaning the blade of my shovel by the creek, I warmed myself by the supper fire, pondering a raw potato that I was lucky enough to stumble across. Bake it? Boil it? I didn't have a pot. Fry it? It was all up to me.

Sitting there—I got an uneasy feeling that something or someone was watching me. Looking around, I glanced across the stream. Rising slowly,

I reached for my rifle. I could see shiny eyes in the shaded darkness of a coyote hole.

Caught staring, knowing he had been spotted, the old prospector elbowed his way out of his sleeping hole, not once taking his eyes off me or my potato. A raggedy man—gaunt, bent with hungry eyes fixed on my potato, splashed across the rivulet spoutin' gibberish and sat down in my company.

Eyeing the spud, he edged up closer and closer. He got so close I was catching his fleas and wearing his cologne. He was in an odd way. Before he sat in my lap, I put the potato down on a rock, halved it with my shovel and handed him half my supper.

Smiling he said, "Looky here." He took a spoon out of his overalls and feebly scooped out a large curl from his half of the potato. Reaching out, he asked me for the shovel. And then from the cuff of his pants he took a pinch of dusty gravel and sprinkled it onto the shovel, mixing it with what he explained later was mercury. He covered the sticky mixture in the hollow of his potato. Swinging the shovel my way, "Put yours on board," and I did.

While holding the shovel on the hot coals cooking our supper, he did his explaining, "Fire melts the amalgam and turns the mercury to vapor, which is leached off up into the baking potato leaving behind the gold."

The curl looked done and so did supper. Resting the shovel on a rock, the potatoes cooled down. Flipping over his potato he gleed, "Magic!" Sure enough there was a button of gold. He flashed a big toothless smile, "Two for one, gold and supper." Admiring his magic he said, "Pick it up, feel the weight."

Stuck to the shovel, I freed it up with a stick and picked up the warm metal. Flipping it around in my hand, it did have some heft. "Good trick," I said, handing the gold back to him.

"Keep it. Thank you for supper." We talked around for a while until he began to nod off. Watching him, I saw he had the bright eyes of a young man, yet he was old and weathered with heavy thoughts. He was asleep.

A night owl hooted and he was awake. "Gettin' late," he yawned. "I'm done in. Appreciate your company. I'll be packin' out in the mornin'." Rising slowly, he left me with, "You may want to think about leavin' too. This place just sands you down and fades your soul. . . 'Night."

"'Night, Birdy." I watched him leave. He turned, mustered a smile and walked, splashing away.

The next morning, I found him across the stream, slumped up against a tree. His cold blue eyes glistened—he was gone.

Placing the last of the big rocks to cover the old prospector in his sleeping hole, I used my shovel and filled in with gravel. Satisfied it looked natural and he would rest in peace, I got on my pony and grabbed up my shovel. Turning to go, I took one last look over the creek and down at the rocks, "Rest your soul, sir," and I wandered off.

Sparks and Fuses

MINING TOWNS sprang up overnight and just as fast turned to dust before building a church or a jail.

Panned out, I decided to head for the mines in the hills. My job was to haul the ore carts in and out of the mine and empty the honey wagon.

For a ten hour shift each man was given four stubby candles to light his work in the drifts and tunnels of the mine. The candles didn't last for ten hours. So at lunch break twenty-five men blew out their candles and we ate, coughing in the infinite blackness of our tomb to save wax.

Having just switched out an ore cart, I was lowered by lift into the throat of the mine. Creaking deeper and deeper into the pitch-black hole, I lit my candle and placed it on the honey wagon. Striking the floor of the shaft and about to enter the tunnel, I heard what I thought was the sound of swarming bees. Impossible, I thought.

I slowly rolled the honey wagon down the track past the glow of candles lighting up the dusty, sweaty faces of the miners and their work. Swinging ten-pound sledgehammers, punching holes and drilling tunnels through miles of rock, inch-by-inch, to collect gold hived in the veins of the earth was back-breaking work. So why were they smiling at me?

I began to feel like the canary in a sandbox of cats.

The hum filled the black tunnel as I rolled by the miners. Aiden, an Irish boy with red hair and my friend, stepped from the darkness into the candlelight. His violin was the source of the swarm. He smiled, bowing one long humming note, and winked. He could play the fiddle better than the devil himself.

He whipped into a hearty melody that inspired and lifted our spirits. The hammer men picked up on the beat. Boom . . . Boom . . Boom. The music of the fiddle filled the mine and rolled over on itself echoing through the tunnels and the shafts. The hammers banged out the beat on the rock walls, cart rails and timbers of the mine. Boom . . . Boom . . Boom.

The miners were ready for play. If they didn't have a hammer they stomped their boots, clapped their hands or played their spoons. I could hear the swishing, side-by-side rhythm of pebbles on a metal sieve as I rolled by.

I pushed the honey wagon down the track. One of the miners jumped on the rolling wagon, swinging his hammer from side to side pounding on it like a big steel drum, Boom . . . Boom . . Boom. The low booming beats vibrated off the tunnel walls in concert with the fiddle. It was unbelievably beautiful.

"Walker," someone called out.

Boom . . . Boom . . Boom.

"I'm coming."

"Walker."

Boom . . . Boom . . Boom.

My name was the verse, called out and thrown from miner to miner from one end of the mine to the other.

"Walker."

Boom . . . Boom . . Boom.

Their faces glowed and their performance overwhelmed me. Pushing the honey wagon to a stop, I noticed the burning fuses. The sparks from the hissing fuses raced to the explosive charges stuffed in the blasting holes of the tunnel. The men quickly backed off covering their heads with shovels. The fiddle played the funeral dirge. The miners watched, enjoying my panic. And, just when I was about to run, Bear Creek Joe, the powder man, snatched the fuses out of the blasting holes in the wall and handed them over to me.

I'd been played. They were all laughing. Aiden stepped forward and with a final flourish of the fiddle, and altogether with whistles, cheers and clapping, the miners shouted, "Happy Birthday."

Quite taken by their opera, I stood there speechless holding the burning fuses sparking in my hand. Overcome with emotion I managed to say, "Thank you."

"Let's eat!" they shouted. And then they all returned to their stations and blew out their candles.

I was sixteen.

Miss Pretty

LIVING UNDERGROUND drilling rock, picking rock, blasting rock, timbering rock, mucking rock, and hauling rock with mules pulling ore carts out of the throats of mines, deep in the veins of the earth, was very dangerous work. The mines were widow-makers.

For fifty cents a day more, Aiden and I moved over and took jobs in the Miss Pretty Mine. On this one day in spring, I had just dumped a load of crushed rock and mine tailings. I was trailing a balky mule, pulling an empty ore cart back up the steep tracks about to enter into the Miss Pretty. The frayed hemp tow rope snapped unleashing the cart. The heavy steel ore cart was on me in a flash, flipping me up, end over tea kettle into the cart.

The cart was rollin', building up speed, clickety-clack, racing down the rails, dropping faster and faster.

Blurring past men and equipment, the 'runaway' rattled, wobbling from side to side, screeching, sparking, squealing and quickly running out of track.

The whole circus happened in a flash, but to me it was an eternity. At this raging speed, I thought, I'd be crashing through the Pearly Gates or racing into the flames of hell before I'm dead.

The shovelmen and teamsters at the base of the mountain looked up and gawked as my iron missile, running out of track, left the earth, smashing through the railings at the end of the loading scaffolding. "Load in flight. Gangway!" I heard them shout. The shadow of the streaking cart struck their faces. In fear, they scrambled for their lives.

And then, silence.

The cart launched upward and soared through the sky on its way to my next divide with such speed the front end lifted as the back end dropped. And, as in a dream, time stood still. The cart slowly turned a complete loop-de-loop in mid-air.

Weightless, I felt I was about to turn inside out.

Falling back to earth, the cart plunged into the pile of crushed rock—BOOM! The report of the impact echoed, trembling like cannon fire striking its mark.

In a storm of dust, the miners rushed over to view my twisted corpse. They leaned in over my body, stiffly wedged and encased in the steel coffin.

Stunned and dazed I slowly opened my eyes as the dust cleared. Blurred by the blazing rays of sunlight, I looked up at the glaring eyes of dark, sweaty faces gawking and hovering over me.

Breathless and in shock, I asked, "Has my soul landed in heaven or crashed in the devil's dust in hell?"

Flaming Arrows

I WAS BROKE and my poke was flat. After more than a year, I hadn't found Ginny and her family in the gold fields and they weren't in Wickenburg. I was on my way to Phoenix to look for her. It was late in the day as I rode along on a narrow Indian trail. I wasn't looking so good. Tired, worn out, wrecked up and starving, I was dying out there.

The trail down from the mine wove and meandered through the mountains where the clouds appeared close enough to reach out and touch. I was playing my mouth music, traveling through narrow outcroppings on both sides of the trail. My pony, picking his way over slippery rock, balked and slowed. I thought it was on account of the rough terrain.

Boy, was I wrong.

I passed through a rock entrance into a small hidden clearing and came face to face with Indian boys with rifles and arrows pointed at all the important parts of me. I should have smelled their smoke. I had come upon their camp.

Facing off, they were a striking composite of feathers, beads, leather and fur. I looked into the eyes of the closest Indian. He cocked his rifle. As I slowly turned my head, looking at each of their faces, I could see a lever cocking or an arrow being drawn back over a bow. I thought it best not to look at the last fellow, knowing that after the last hammer was cocked, there was only one thing left for them to do.

My eyes drifted back to the first brave. His rock-hard expression began to crumble. His eyes brightened and a broad smile lit up his face. He began to laugh, yes he did. They can laugh. He disengaged the hammer of his rifle and as he did, his brothers looked over at him in wonder. He pointed to a small trailside chain fruit cholla cactus. He made a motion as if he's holding one of the thorny fruits in his hand and touched it to different parts of his body, and then smiled, pointing to me.

Well, pretty soon the joke's on me. They all laughed and lowered their rifles and arrows. These were the very same Tonto Apache Indian boys who were going to ambush our wagons and had watched me crash into the giant cholla cactus. I was the boy who dances with pain.

The beef was on the fire and they fed me pretty good. We had few words in common but we were able to communicate well enough with hand gestures and drawings in the dirt. I told them I had crossed the ocean in a big ship and crossed the prairie in a boat on wheels, a prairie schooner. I think they understood.

They told me about Mother Earth and the buffalo, and how their fathers' fathers' fathers hunted this land with bows and arrows, and now are being pressed from the West.

I felt their sorrow. My eyes found it hard to meet theirs. It was a moment of silence that held us all—staring deep into the fire. A pause of reflection that begged the question: why is this boundless land of endless horizon not big enough for all the people? Are we not fingers on the same hand? The flames sparked and snapped and we were back.

We sat around the fire. They were fascinated by my mouth music. They grinned and laughed watching me puff and wiggle my fingers, cupping the shiny Hohner. Gesturing, I held it out to the leader, Blue Tail. Surprised, he backed off, waving his hands, 'no'. The others laughed and I laughed right along. Sitting closest to me, Loose Arrow decided he'd give it a go and extended his hand. I handed it to him. He held the harmonica carefully between his thumbs and forefingers. He slowly put it to his lips and blew. His breath screeched a piercing cord. Startled, he dropped it like a hot potato. We all laughed and then passed the harmonica around the fire taking turns huffing and puffing out a melody.

Enjoying their company, I remembered the parting gift given to me by the pallbearers at my mock funeral, celebrating the blessed moment of my divine revival. The miners gave me a bottle of red-eye to warm me up on cold nights on the trail. And when things got rough, I might want to take a nip.

Well, we passed the bottle around. We were all about the same age, sixteen and seventeen—firing up. The music started to sound better, actually quite good for beginners. This was the first time I'd taken a drink and judging from what happened, it appeared it was their very first time as well. Pretty soon we were all laughing, acting silly, and dancing.

We watched the clouds in the sky tear themselves on the mountain peaks. They appeared to be closing in on us. The Indians picked up their bows and pierced the dried, fallen fruits of cholla cactus with their arrows and held them to the fire. Drawing back their flaming arrows, they shot them straight up into the night sky. Their arrows blazed upward, whistling with streaming fire, piercing the clouds. The clouds bloomed with fire and glowed from the inside, like lightning sparking up. It was quite an amazing sight to behold.

We did this over and over and shared our song into the night.

About to Crow

THE NEXT MORNING at sunrise, four Indian boys and I stood at the edge of the largest cattle range I'd ever seen. Friends, we made our signs and said our goodbyes. They rode off into the West. I'm pretty sure I heard them laughing as they rode away. Oh, what a night.

Just off the horizon I gazed at the morning star, Venus. The palo verde trees and cactus flowers of springtime were abloom. I sat there on my Indian pony looking over the vast landscape and the colors of fire in the sky. My heart swelled and my eyes widened, feeling the grandeur before me. It was at that moment I realized even though I didn't know where I was going, I was not lost.

Enjoying the moment, I was surprised when I heard, "Howdy." Silently, a rider rode up alongside me. "Beautiful isn't it?" he commented, staring straight ahead.

"Yes. The Almighty used up all the good stuff when He created this. I was just about to crow."

The cowboy laughed.

Some men just look like cowboys—fit in the saddle, tall and lean, with an inner quality of strength and character measured beyond physical. I had just met that cowboy. "You lost?" he asked.

"No, sir. Just taking it all in."

"What are you doin' out here in the middle of God's country?"

"I don't know—passing through." Pausing, I said, "Thinking."

"Of where you've been or where you're goin'?"

"Both. The future mostly. What's done is done."

"The desert's a good place to be at sunrise, taking measure of oneself." And, as if measuring me, he said, "Destiny is a constant companion."

"I better watch out for tomorrow then, 'cause mine's off to a pretty shaky start."

Smiling he inquired, "Where are your folks?"

I pointed and looked up. "They left me early."

"Any family?"

"No. Almost."

Well, the cowboy and I talked for a spell. I told him about meeting and losing the love of my heart, "Like the sun, she made me shine," and about our abrupt parting on the trail. "I was left with this keepsake. I wear it in my pocket." Reaching into my shirt, I held up Ginny's pearl button for him to see.

Getting comfortable, we just sat there yakking as the sun greeted the day. I told him about my adventures. He especially liked the part about the devil's hogs from hell. "Yes sir, I was close enough to smell the smoke and feel the fire." He laughed. Then I got to laughing.

Taking a set in the saddle he said, "There's nothing like sunshine, the open range and living the coarse, sparse life of a cowboy to clear your head and discover your mettle. You'll be good at it."

Smiling, I asked, "Why so?"

"You have spirit," he said, "I can see it in your heart." He paused, "And, I like the way you crow." He broke into a broad smile. "Ride on up to the ranch house in Seven Springs and ask the old man if you can ride for his brand."

"Ranch house?"

The cowboy gestured like it was just over yonder.

I didn't see anything but miles of rocky, rolling hills, desert range and cattle. I turned back, just about to ask him how to get there when he gestured, "Follow that peak. Good luck." With that, he picked up his reins and moved off. "And don't let the old man tell you he's full up. He's always got room for a good man."

"Thank you, sir. Say, who should I say sent me?"

Without turning, he answered, "Sunny. . . And be sure to give him my heartfelt hello." Riding away, Sunny asked, "What's your sweetheart's name?"

"Ginny. Ginny Hart."

I watched him turn into a shadow against the rising sun. His voice trailed off as he repeated, "Give him my heartfelt hello."

The Old Man

SO I STARTED OFF at a jiggle with an eye on the peak playing a tinny tune on my harmonica. I rode all day. And just as I started thinking I was lost, there was the ranch house.

I arrived just before sunset, passing a couple of roughs leaving through the gate as I was riding in. I heard them grousing, "That old crow couldn't tell a top hand from a fence post." Eyeing me, they snarled as they passed by, "Forget it, kid."

There was no missing the old man. Wearing a high-crown Stetson, he was charging out of the ranch house as I rode up. A man framed-up tall of rough timber that with age had slumped and settled comfortably around the middle. He had a handsome face with a salted grey mustache. His eyes were wise with a look of frontier hardship. I approached him with a, "Good day, sir."

He read me at a glance, "We're full up."

"There's always room for a good man, sir." He stopped in his tracks and then I said exactly what Sunny told me to say, "I'm looking to ride for your brand."

"You a cowboy?" he asked with a big booming voice.

"Not yet, sir," sounding like an unoiled hinge.

"Can you rope?"

"No, sir," shaking my head.

"Good with a knife?"

"No, sir," shaking my head.

"Do you have a knife?"

Shaking my head no.

"Shoe a horse?"

Shaking my head.

"Can you shoot?"

Still shaking my head.

"You handy with tools?"

Shaking no.

"Can you cook?"

Shaking no.

"You drink?"

"Just once, sir. I liked it."

His cold eyes measured me. "Well, you're not a liar. Praise the Lord. Boy, what can you do?"

Feeling lower than a snake, I reached into my pocket and pulled out my harmonica. "I'm workin' on my song."

Hard looking, he didn't laugh. Finished with me, he started walking off in a hurry, saying over his shoulder, "Sorry, son, but the outfit's full-handed. I just filled the last two bunks this morning."

Turning to leave, I remembered what Sunny told me. I charged right over to him, slid off, dropped the reins and my pony stopped dead. I caught the old man by surprise and gave him a big heartfelt hug. And before he could haul off and—I said, "Sir, Sunny told me when I see you I was to give you his heartfelt hello. . . Hello."

Taken aback, the old man just gazed at me. "You met up with Sunny?" His eyes fixed on me. "How'd he look?"

"Yes, sir, he looked fine and fit on the range this morning."

The old man began to smile, a slow smile that started deep from inside and brightened his face.

Thinking that's that, I swung back up onto my pony and turned to go. "Well, thank you, sir."

Raising his Stetson and running his hand through his hair he pointed, "The bunkhouse is over there. You can begin learnin' to be a cowboy by closing the gate. Earnin' your keep starts tomorrow at sunup."

I rode over and closed the gate.

The Cook

THE NEXT MORNING, I sat there in the dark waiting on the sun. I was about to learn that once you signed on, you stood by your pards and defended the outfit. If things didn't work out, you were free to drift. But until that time, you gave your word and you lived up to it. And that was that.

Being new, I wrangled the firewood, the water and washed all the dishes. I loaded the chuck wagon's possum-belly with kindling, greased the axles, harnessed the mules and rode drag, choking in the dust. The days were hot, dry and long. When work needed to be done, I was at the head of the line.

Hatchet, the outfit's cook, was recovering from a nasty spill, and asked the old man for a helper for the cattle drive. The old man obliged him, but said his cook's wages of two and a half dollars a day would be cut to a dollar and half per day. Hatchet said that would do. The old man was a businessman. He got two men for the price of one. He paid me with the dollar he saved on the cook.

Up before light, I built the cook fire and got the coffee going. I soon learned cooking for the outfit was more than boiling water. Mixing, flipping, rolling, frying, roasting and smoking, Hatchet had it down. He could batch together a feast fit for kings. Mmmm, I still can taste his fancy fluff-duffs.

The old man had ranch chickens and a milk cow. He liked milk in his coffee. On roundups and drives, we traveled the chickens and left the cow at the ranch.

The cook was also the medicine man. For cuts, bruises, bites, gores and toothaches, he had a variety of potions and lotions on board the 'cookie box.' That's what he called his chuck wagon.

"Keep lookin'. It's in there somewhere," shouted Hatchet. I was rooting around the shelves shuffling about the Epsom salts, calomel, kerosene oil, vinegar, arnica, salve, quinine and mustang liniment. No whiskey was allowed on the trail.

"Try a drawer," pressed Hatchet.

In the first drawer I opened, I spied a tintype likeness of a handsome young couple dressed up in their frills and finest. I'm sure it was Hatchet and his lady. In all the time we rode together he never spent any words on her, but I often saw him gaze upon her in the light of the lantern, forlorn and missing her in the night. I was missing Ginny.

Hatchet was tending to a cowboy sitting on a box

with a terrible toothache. The boy was holding his swollen jaw moaning in awful pain. "Think about swishing around some water after meals, boy. A little vinegar water once in awhile, would be a good idea," advised the doc.

"Found 'em!" Hatchet had a pair of pliers, angled and filed down for pulling rotten teeth.

Muffled in throbbing pain, the patient mumbled, "Ya can yank 'em all doc if 'n it'll stop the pain."

Yes sir, Hatchet was the watch that kept things ticking. With his good nature and reputation for tasty vittles, the outfit was never short handed. He was the reason many of them hired on.

On drives, I was up in the morning at three, working around the fire and stiff sleeping cowboys, some who had just gotten' off night watch and would be up at quarter past five to gobble breakfast.

The glow of a lantern would light up the chuck wagon. Hatchet was in the habit of talking to himself as he cooked. "With a cup of flour, a pinch of this, a dab of that," interrupting himself, "Helper, put two Dutch ovens on the coals." Visualizing the quantity needed and the measurements of the ingredients, he unconsciously calculated with his thumb and his fingers, "Two, three, four, six, seven. . ."

While preparing one dish, he would have me working on another. "Helper, grab up sixteen potatoes, cut out the dark spots and chop 'em up fine," and he'd be right back to his fixin's. "With just the right amount of shortening and half a pour of what's in this bottle."

"What's in that bottle? I asked.

Hatchet just smiled not about to divulge Merlin's

secret potion. "Crack open eight eggs, and whip 'em in a bowl." He taught me how to make a dandy boggy-top, a pie washed down with a hot cup of Arbuckles', leaving the cowboys wanting more.

Breakfast was a commotion of cowboys and wranglers coming and going; gobbling down chuck; packing up gear; loading the chuck wagon and riding out to drive the herd. And all the while Hatchet made it look easy.

Right after breakfast we snapped the reins and rolled the mules out. Seeing a cowboy's war bag and hot roll still spread out on the ground, I was about to jump off the wagon and load it on. Hatchet stopped me and said, "Leave it. It ain't that waddy's first time."

We hurried on so we could set up for lunch and rendezvous with the outfit half way up the trail.

Gathering, rounding up and pushing a string of two thousand head of wild-eyed and spooky cattle up the trail while riding green broncs was a dangerous stunt. With thrashing tails, bobbing horns and tramping hooves, the sudden sound of a hack or cough or flighty shadow could set the herd off into a frenzy—a cowboy's nightmare—Stampede!

The heaving mass of cattle kicked up an endless rolling cloud of dust as they snailed along ten to fifteen miles before nightfall.

Road runners darted and raced alongside the chuck. I looked over the open range at the distant horizon. In the lead, it was our job to scout for water, find a campground and be prepared to greet the outfit with a hot meal for supper.

Hatchet reminded me of the captain of a ship.

A pilot with a good sense of direction, he had a compass in his head.

We hardly ever butchered our own cattle, usually it was another man's brand. It didn't matter none, he butchered one of ours right back, so it all evened up. Or, we would hunt wild game. Riding along looking off over the range, Hatchet reined up the mules, Sally and Rocky. "Hand me the carbine." I handed him the Springfield. "See it?"

"Good eye." A mule deer was hidden in the mesquites. I was impressed.

From the seat of the wagon Hatchet drew up slowly, taking careful aim. "Take a breath…aaand squeeze." With a cloud of smoke, he dropped the buck in its tracks. "Meat tonight! Cowboys' delight."

Hatchet didn't say much. He banked his words and saved them for when they counted. "That's our spot up ahead. Water—a cocktail for a thirsty herd, good grazing, plenty of firewood and we'll be out of the way."

We had been zigzagging up and down, all around all day. I looked over the immeasurable vastness of the open range. "You sure they'll find us?"

"Oh, I'm pretty sure they'll find us alright. Between the water and our smoke, they'll just follow their noses. I haven't lost a herd yet." He rolled the wagon up to a stop. "Take this sixty-footer." He handed me a *reata*, "Loop it around that dead stump, stretch it out and fasten a stick to the other end. And, scribe me a circle in the dirt."

With that done, Hatchet positioned the cookie box in the center of the circle and matter-of-factly told me, "Your last chore tonight is when the stars come out be sure to point the tongue of the wagon in the direction of the North Star so the old man will have a sense for which way to head the cattle out in the morning. Don't forget." Everything was matter-of-fact and easy with Hatchet, until you forgot—I didn't forget. How could I? Every night when I pointed the wagon towards the North Star, I thought of Ginny. I enjoyed the last chore of the day.

I unhitched the mules, lowered the flapboard, and set up the poles to stretch the chuck's canvas fly for shade and we got to cooking. I was hungry.

"Wrangle up some water, enough for drinkin' now and coffee in the morning. By the time them cows top off tonight, that water will be beef tea and plenty tough."

The Dutch ovens were on the coals and the venison was slowly roasting. Over a cup of coffee Hatchet made his joke, "What's WB stand for? White Beans?" Smiling, from one cook to another I enjoyed his company and his recipe.

My job was to keep the stew from boiling and turn and baste the roast. "Slather that good sauce all over."

Then Hatchet unveiled 'the crock.' "The secret to sourdough is in the age of the starter." My mouth watered. He guarded that crock of starter like it was family. And, with reflective pause, "This starter was passed on to me at Gettysburg from a cook whose grandfather scavenged it from a fleeing British regiment on the run in 1776—yeast, flour, sugar and potato water to feed the fermenting yeast—this is alive and requires a watchful eye. Never use all of it and always replace what you use."

While rolling balls of soft dough in the palms

of his hands, Hatchet shared some trailside wisdom which he was prone to do from time to time. "We got new hands on this drive and they can do, and be, whatever they want out there. But within this kitchen circle, they'll mind their manners."

Sure enough late in the afternoon we could see the rising canopy of dust from the cattle. Smelling the water, the bellowing herd was coming on.

Hungry from the tasty aromas of the baking, boiling and sizzlin' fixin's, I was ready to eat the smoke.

The cattle were all watered and grazing. It was time for supper. "Get ready, White Beans," said Hatchet. "Here comes hungry."

Well, right off, blazin' in, I could see it coming. The race was on. Two cowhands, Eddy and Barlow, were dashin' and splashin' in for grub. I looked over at the cook, he was on simmer. The two breezed into the circle dragging dust. We watched as their dust floated over the Dutch ovens, stew pots and the roast. They tied off their horses to the wheels of the chuck wagon and stepped to the head of the line.

If you want to see who's in charge, start something with the cook.

Hatchet stepped forward with a smile, "What can I do for you, boys?"

"We's hungry dawgs! Hoowl! Hoowl! How..."

And before they could finish their howl, the cook comes to a boil, rapping on their chests with the big kettle spoon, backing them down and out of the circle. "You stampeded into my chuck, dusting my ovens and pots, glazing my fine roast with dirt. Have you no manners?"

The boys sputtered and stuttered.

Shaking the spoon, he pointed down to the line in the dirt circling his empire and said, "Don't cross that line without asking my permission first. In the future, and that means right now, before you ask for that privilege, think about rubbin' up, dust yourselves off, wash your hands and face and rake your hair before you come up to dine at my banquet table. And furthermore, the next time you blaze on in here and tie off your horse to the wheel of my chuck, I'm cookin' it."

Watching from a safe distance, the whole outfit stood off, glad it wasn't them facing up to the spoon. His point made, and knowing he had the full choir's attention, Hatchet turned to the outfit, "And, one more thing. If you waddies want to sleep in your hot roll tonight, make sure you roll it up in the morning and stuff it into the wagon. It's a long ride back."

That was the law. . . and order.

Rockin' and Roastin'

ISIDORO, A SPANISH CALIFORNIO and older than the rest of the outfit, could remember a story like it was book-read. Being that none of the boys had ever opened the door to a schoolhouse, when 'el Book' told a story around the campfire, we were all up front. With good English and the flair of a Spanish accent, he told of romantic memories passed down through the generations of the caballeros and vaqueros of his family.

El Book knew horses.

"*Amigos! Muchachos!* Buckaroos! What I tell you is true. *Dios* created the *caballo*—the horse— magnificent spirited animals of beauty, grace and speed—royal mounts fit for the pleasures of kings and queens.

Charles V, Holy Roman Emperor, King of Spain,

looking to expand his empire, and with rumors of gold and riches in the new world, dispatched an armada of sailing ships, heavy with guns and huge white canvas sails that rose to capture the high winds and imaginations of early explorers.

Daring to cross the endless horizon of crashing waves and bottomless ocean, Hernán Cortés, with sixteen caballos on board—very fine they looked—landed his eleven Spanish ships in Vera Cruz in 1519. They were the first horse tracks on the new world.

Cortés harbored his ships and anchored offshore. Then he and his men waited for the moonlight. They crossed the water riding the swimming horses ashore. They were armed with sticks that thundered and fired lightning. The Indians had never seen a horse or firearms before and were frightened thinking these intruders—men upon horses—were beasts from the sea with two heads and six legs.

The Indians fled into the jungle. And in the days that followed, they watched from the shadows as the intruders burned their own ships in a great blaze."

Captivated by el Book's performance, our ears were sponges, our eyes bugged out and our jaws dropped.

"Their medicine men were not able to ward off this evil magic." With lyrical gestures, el Book shuffled around the fire stirring up the flames, "All their dancing and singing and all their smoke did not stop the ships from arriving with more horses.

"As time went on, these eleven stallions and five mares, Arabian barbs, strayed, wandered and bred with the other horses forming small bands. These spirited horses survived in spite of the short mountain grasses and semi-arid climate. They became the stunted and sturdy wild mustangs we ride today.

Huge numbers of *vacada*—cattle—bred and endured much like the *caballo*. Roaming the plains and ranges for centuries, they multiplied becoming wild—as wild as deer. These Spanish longhorn cattle arrived in 1521 and so did the *vaqueros*—or as you call them, cowboys."

After three months of choking dust, we were back at the ranch. I was helping Hatchet, who appeared to be fully recovered from his accident, move supplies into the ranch house. The old man didn't miss much, "WB, leave that stuff to Hatchet, he's milked it 'bout long enough. He's going to want a maid tomorrow."

"An' a butler," quipped Hatchet. I put down the box of Arbuckles' coffee and caught up to the old man on his way to the ranch house.

Hatchet called out, "I'll thank you for my dollar a day in wages back, sir."

"Yeah, yeah, yeah," bristled the old man.

The old man always walked like he was on a mission. Turning to me, "It's time to get you on a horse."

I'd never been to the ranch house. Hands stayed in the bunkhouse where we slept, ate, played cards and stored our stuff—whatever we had, and it wasn't much. So when the old man asked me up to the ranch house, I was pretty excited.

"Come on in."

It was the first house I'd been in in three years. The ranch house had real glass windows cut into the adobe walls. Large round peeled timbers supported the ceiling of planks. The hearth was set in the center of a stacked stone fireplace. There were colorful Indian rugs on the floor. A collection of rifles and carbines, Sharps and Spencers, hung on racks along the walls. "Nice house, sir."

The old man went over to a fine, tall cabinet, rummaged around and pulled out a pair of rusty spurs and a knife. "You'll need these."

Looking around, just making conversation, "Sir, have you ever had a notion of doing something other than cowboying?" I had opened a heavy door.

Lifting his eyes, the old man pulled back the spurs. "Son, cowboying is my way of life, the way I live. This is my home, my land, fought and paid for. I live free and fair—my terms, my business."

Looking eye to eye, standing toe to toe for what was to be the longest, most awkward moment of my life, the old man was not finished.

"Cowboying is the hardest, toughest, hottest, coldest, dustiest, wettest, dangerous and most thrilling work I've ever done. And if you're expecting anything different, then you best not put these on."

Sharp as flint, the old man had a way with words and I didn't miss one of them. He expected an answer and he waited for it. Stumped up, I searched for a reply. I looked down at the spurs in his hand. And, after a long, long moment, "Sir, I think they'll fit."

Sitting around the campfire, the outfit made their charge. "Ya lookin' ta trade the shade of the chuck's fly fo' forkin' horses—rockin' and roastin' in the hot sun?" asked Eddy snidely, one of the two cowhands with billy-goat beards, who had faced up to 'the spoon.'

No longer the cook's helper, I was their fair game. Lifting an eye from my plate, looking over the fire and around the circle, I could feel thunder rolling in. The vaqueros and cowboys were sizing up the new button. Eddy slowly drawled, "Brandin' cattle's a ho' lot different than bakin' biscuits, Sovereign. Ya best think 'bout it fo' ya climbs aboard. Cuz if y'all don't cuts it, it's git-git-git alooong lil' dogie—you're on your. . ."

"Blaaah!" bawled Barlow, who always echoed Eddy's voice and finished his song, "way home."

"Th' tenderfoot 'll be trail boss by th' end of th' day!" jested Eddy.

"Trail boss by th' end of th' day," laughed Barlow from his mouth of decay.

Wiping out a dish and not looking over at the prattlers, Hatchet cooled the boiling pot, "I'll be wagerin' on WB's grit over your blow."

Had the boys not favored my desserts, it would have been full-out laughter. As it was, they just winked around and snickered.

Restless, I awakened early the next morning, anxious to get started and ate with Hatchet. Lifting a fork, the cook served up his recipe, "Just stay on your horse."

"That's it?"

"Pretty much. If you have it in you, you'll find it. And, if you don't, they'll see it."

Scraping my plate clean, I laughed, "Stay on my horse?"

"Yep."

I put my dishes in the wash tub, mounted up and rode out alone, easing into the darkness.

In the solitude of the morning, admiring the majesty of the sunlit haze rising on the snowcapped peaks of the purple mountains, I was filled by the awesome power of a sunrise glowing over the fertile range, running free from the horizon in all directions.

The Indian embraced Mother Earth, realizing their oneness of spirit from their very beginning. I was feeling that spirit and discovering my dream. And before I grew old, I would experience both.

I joined the round-up of wild range cattle scattered and hidden in the arroyos and ridges of the distant landscape. My joy and observation were harshly interrupted by assaults to my nature dealt daily by stiff company. The cutlery of their barbs and biting jest belittled and made me feel the fool.

Apparently Eddy's thirty mile round-about retrieving his forgotten bedroll gave him time enough to grow dislike for the cook and now harvest his revenge on the cook's helper.

It got rough fast.

Once after dinner, I was mounted up waiting on the outfit. Without me noticing, Barlow snuck around and put a prickly pear fruit under my horse's tail. His immediate performance made for the mid-day amusement and pleasure of the outfit. My horse went to pitching and bucking and hopping around the camp; stomping on the fire, scattering the hands; flipping over the coffee pot and pans; tearing down the fly on the chuck wagon and flap-jacking me into the wild blue yonder.

Eddy was well liked, with a quick lip. He inspired the cowhands' relentless parade of insults and sport with me. Whatever I did or had to say fell on deaf ears or was fodder for ridicule. With tone and temper they made me feel small.

Grey skies and muddy water came over me, shaping my thinking. My temper ran afoul. I slipped into melancholy and turned inward.

Long days were followed by longer nights. I was riding night watch on the herd of wild cattle we were readying to sort-out and trail brand. I could hear Eddy and the laughter of the hands around the campfire.

In the habit of making unexpected visits, the old man silently rode up beside me circling the herd, "Beautiful night."

"Yes, sir, it truly is."

"Doing more than your share of night guard?"

"Better than feeding the cackle around the fire." I was ready to rip.

"Kind'a sour are ya'?"

"Sir, I'm looked upon as an empty vessel, not fit to hold reins, barely able to ride the wood!"

The old man answered me as if he hadn't captured my mood.

"How's the knee and leg control coming along?"

"Real good, sir. It's makin' a big difference."

"And the spur touches?"

"Big difference."

"The boys you're riding with have those skills, son. Had 'em since they were bitty. Vaqueros were held in the arms of their papas and rocked to sleep while riding the rhythm of a walking horse. Cowboys were whirling and dropping their strings on the rooster while collecting eggs for momma."

Turning to me with a smile he continued, "They're not about to let a greenhorn ride with the outfit without tuning him up." He paused, "It's time to come out of the shade, boy. Force and resistance are the same thing. If you got it, give it."

Letting his words set in, he told me, "Go on and get some rest. You're going to need it in the morning. I'll take the watch."

Chewing on the old man's words, I was put off. Just about to say something, I bit my lip and drifted off leaving the old man watching my back. "Night, sir."

Mulling over his words, I rode back to camp, jumped into my bag and went to sleep.

The corrals were a swirling chaos of colors and 'loco' motion with hair-raising hides, powerful hooves and whirling sharp horns in a constant trumpet of lowing, blatting, snorting and bellowing.

I plunged in with all the enthusiasm of an empty sack, worried this would be the end of me.

Blinded by the smothering dust, smoke and sweat, the perils of working on foot and being gored, bit, kicked and stomped went on day after day. We roped and tossed animals struggling to bust free, bawling in pain from our branding irons and ear marks in what appeared to me to be Lucifer's playground.

And yet, day after day, there was not a scrappier lot of good-humored pranksters—mostly at my expense. More than one time, while I waited to drop the next calf, all the loops of every cowhand's lariat found me, laying me out to roll in the dust of their laughter. Their rough company did not crease or fold me. Try as they may, I did not buck. If they scratched for a weakness, my hide stayed intact.

I had ignored Eddy's increasing assaults to my humor in attempt to provoke me. It was late in the day and the hands were spent. The smells of supper wafted over and mixed with the stale singed stench of branding. Barlow was picking up and I was pulling the irons from the hot coals of the branding fire.

The corrals were near empty. Wild with room to run, the few remaining steers were hostile, nervous and threatening.

All day in the sweltering heat, Eddy had been needling, "Columbus! Be careful of those tender hands of yours with those hot, heavy, heavy irons."

A line of punchers clearing the corrals yelled and fanned their hats moving the ornery steers back out to the open range.

Eddy was working over the branding chute, a narrow passage of poles and rails that ran alongside the corral allowing twenty cattle, head-to-tail, to enter at a time. Eddy kept gnawing at me with his jaw-flappin' lip. "What's I got t' do t' release your wolf —so I can skin your hide? Brand your 'sweet-tart's' pearly button to your forehead?"

"Ooow," howls Barlow mouthing his base nature, "Sweet-tart."

Enough's enough, "Eddy, why don't you bring that hot mouth of yours over here and I'll brand it up nice an' purdy fo' ya! And, I'll clip your ears back."

Cracking his knuckles, "Ti yi yo, be right over, dogie." With a gust of wind, Eddy's hat flipped off and sailed into the chute. He jumped down to retrieve it.

It happened in a tick. A savage bull whirled, breaking back through the line of arm-wavers, scattering the punchers and charged into the open end of the chute.

Startled and penned-in, Eddy saw the raging bull. Terror gripped his face. He glanced wide-eyed over at me through the rails.

I watched the chute rumble and shake. Racking from side to side, the furious bull focused on Eddy. With flaring nostrils, the bull lowered his head for ram.

Struck by the action, I grabbed up a smoldering branch of firewood and wheeled, thrusting it into the chute across the poles just as the horns of the bull's head slammed into it, ripping it from my hands, snapping it like a matchstick, showering Eddy with sparks.

Shuttering dust from end to end, the chute creaked. I winced and the cowhands gasped, as the log splintered, but held just inches from a shaking Eddy. A hanging ember sparked singeing Eddy's billy-goat beard. Dazed, the bull bellowed releasing his slobbering drool, spraying Eddy.

Eddy didn't rush to thank me, but the slings and arrows stopped. And a new rawhide, worthy of their company with a nature they could depend on, joined the fire and laughter of their circle.

Being that Eddy had only one shirt, he took a lot of tease wearing it. Everyday he'd lose a little more cotton. Peppered with spark holes, by the end of summer, 'Sparky' was riding shirtless.

Cowboying

STANDING IN THE SHADOWS of the vaqueros, I had kept my ears cocked. I thought it best to model my performance. My eyes drank in everything. I watched the knacks of the wranglers and the ways of the cowboys. Up before the sun and last in the saddle at night, I worked hard and learned fast, honing my skills. I learned where to be and when to be there.

I picked up Spanish pretty good listening to el Book's stories and made a special effort to learn the language of the Indian and his signs for when we pass trails in the future.

Roping was an art. The vaqueros were masters. They could rope a snake. Coordinating distance with the speed and running power of a steer with the speed of your horse required perfect timing.

I learned to whirl a sixty foot *reata*—rope.

Galloping full-out, pitching a long cast, placing the *lazo*—loop—under the steer's feet at the exact moment they came off the ground and with the catch, set up my horse for the shock; and taking the slack out of the rope while wrapping a couple quick dallies around the saddle horn without losing a finger or a thumb, took practice. I got good at it.

Got so when I loosened the thong and shook out a loop, my horse knew we were going to the dance. Maintaining position, avoiding a side pull and facing the animal, he kept a constant tug.

The old man took his time, showing me the how-to-dos. He put a real brainy cutter in my string. The cutter made me look good. When a steer had to be cut from the herd for any reason—branding, sale or doctoring—we'd start slow and easy, quietly urging the steer to the outside of the herd. And with a sudden dash, the steer was separated. When the steer tried to rejoin the herd, my horse anticipated his every move. With speed and action, we could spin and turn faster than the steer.

The old man taught me how to shoot and he showed me how to hunt. I remember the first time I fired a shotgun. We were out along the piñon pines. He was anxious to try out two brand-new, out-of-the-crate, Remington and Sons ten-gauge double barrels. Keeping the wind on our side, I got so I could drop wild game with every pop.

Riding back to the ranch house we enjoyed the rewards of the day—wild turkeys swung over the backs of our saddles. Looking down, I noticed the rusty spurs he had given me had polished up to a nice shiny patina.

It had been a while, and I was keeping an eye out for Sunny. One day I reined up alongside the jigger boss and asked, "Say, boss, when will Sunny be comin' in?"

He replied, "You seen 'em too?"

"Yeah. I wanted to thank him for hookin' me up with the outfit."

He told me that Sunny was jigger boss before he got the job, and that Sunny was the old man's son. One day Sunny's riding point on a herd to market when something spooked 'em. They got to rolling quick. When the dust cleared, Sunny was gone. His passing left the old man heartbroken.

"But, I saw Sunny, real as you and me sittin' here."

"On a Spanish mustang, dappled white with patches of gray and black?"

"Yep, the very one."

"Used to be on reports of seeing Sunny, and raising the old man's hopes, we would ride out to search for him. After a while we just gave that up." As we both looked out over the range, he continued, "Oh, Sunny's out there alright. Rimmin' around, ridin' on ridge tops and the high points, lookin' for strays."

He clucked, jingled his spur and rode off. We never spoke of it again.

A Greasy Sack Outfit

WITHOUT REALLY KNOWING, I had built a reputation. Wasn't long before the old man gave me a chance to boss a greasy sack outfit—brush-poppin' cattle and scouring for mustangs in rough country. Terrain too rough for wagons, we ran our food and supplies in on mules and horses.

Every day was a challenge. Rounding up mustangs, I admired their wild freedom. Elusive and smart, they would run for days requiring our persistence and patience. Breaking them, I learned to fly. My landings needed work. Loose and limber, I learned to roll.

Cowboying wasn't all glory—low wages, fleas and gray-backs, toothaches, tough water and lonely nights so cold I'd wake up and run around to thaw out. A lot of these ride-along, jaw-breaking, brag-on weaners just aired their lungs and scattered cattle.

I lost track of time and Ginny. My eighteenth birthday and Christmas came and went.

With just-paid wages, T-Bone, Adam and I rode into town with money to burn.

The town glowed like a beacon in the night and was a welcome distraction after three months on the trail. A loud and rowdy harbor with game, folly and vice, served up to entertain and boost the spirits and wages of the lonesome and trail-weary.

We tied off our horses and with a jingle in our pockets, pushed through the swinging saloon doors into a haze of drifting smoke and wandered over the wooden floor, through a spirited corral of music, dancing and laughter.

Drifters, cowboys and gamblers were engaged in faro, dice and roulette. The action was thick and fast.

In all its raucous gaiety, the reckless hands— touchy as scorpions, were trailin' for trouble—it was 'bout too noisy to bear.

Bellied up to the bar with one foot on the brass rail, we stood in awe staring at the huge oversized painting of a reclining woman, robust in form, revealed in all her splendor.

Blushing, an aberration of delight widened our eyes, when all of a sudden she appeared to breathe and quiver.

The barkeep interrupted our vision, "Ain't she a beauty? What can I get you, boys. . . whiskey, mule punch, bloody gut, mescal?" Grinning at our distraction, waiting for our answer, he asked, "Haven't you boys never seen a naked lady before?"

"No!" we answered.

Leaning in with eyes wide open, "See that!" gestured Adam. "She's breathing again!"

Smiling and without looking at the painting, the barkeep just laughed, "You boys are dreamin'— been out on the trail too long."

"Look! Look!" I pointed, "She's doing it again."

Laughing, the barkeep poured us a whiskey, "This one's on the house, boys." And then I noticed the reflection in a mirror from behind the bar. The barkeep's foot, slow and steady, was squeezing air from a bellows connected to a tube which was snaked up behind the 'breathtaking' painting which explained her lively performance.

Bamboozled, we laughed. This was our night to howl—and howl we did!

Full of folly, we flashed our Colts from the jamboree whoopin'.

Adam had gotten into a rough-and-tumble over something—cards, whiskey, night-blooming flowers—and returned to camp with a fogged eye. From then on, we called him Punch.

T-Bone roostered, slickered and in need of money to cover his losses with Lady Luck, sold me his batwing chaps with the silver *conchos*. He wore 'em to town and I wore 'em back. Real beauties.

Stumbling into the bunkhouse, Punch helped me get T-Bone inside. A lantern spilled its light over a game of cards. The boys weren't smiling and lingered about in their long johns. Cowboys didn't stay around long after the last drive to market.

Raking in the pot, Shakes, one of the wranglers, greeted us, "Welcome back, girls. Been waitin' on ya." The rest of the hands climbed out of their bed rolls. "The old man stopped by, says he's going to miss us." Shuffling the cards, Shakes announced, "Time to cut the cards, boys." Slapping the cards on the table, he knocked the deck, "Jacks or better—ride out."

Glum hands, we cut the cards. Mine was the queen of hearts. "See you in the spring, boys."

I took a day. Parting company with the outfit was hard, but parting company with my Indian pony was even harder, but it was time. The old man said he'd keep an eye on him. I turned him out in good feed. Partners—he had carried me faithfully in good humor all the way across country and to the mines and back—he was ready for pension.

I shod my new rangy sorrel, cleaned my saddle blanket, tied a half hitch with a keeper with the cantle strings around my slicker and I was on my way.

Getting an early start before sunup, I was riding out when I saw the old man squatting by the coffee fire poking the coals. What's he doing up so early? I moseyed over to say my good bye. The old man's face was seamed by sun and toil. He was focused on the flames of the fire.

Without looking up, he poured coffee into a tin cup and handed it to me as I got off my horse. Not lifting his eyes, he just kept stirring the coals. "Good coffee, sir." I said. No response. He's fixed on the altar of the fire. Well, standing around with distant company I finished my coffee. "I'll be on my way." I bent down to set my cup on the fire pit rock, "Thank you, sir. I sure appreciate all you've done for me."

Still not turning to face me he said, "You did real good, cowboy." As I stood up, so did he. With wet eyes he gave me a hug, "You did real good, son."

It was an emotional moment that had us both drying an eye. Enough said. I swung aboard and he went back to poking the fire.

As I rode away, I heard the old man's final words. "Next time you see Sunny, give him my heartfelt hello."

"Yes, sir. I surely will."

I closed the gate on my way out.

A Lonesome Go

LEAVING THE OLD MAN was the second hardest thing I'd ever had to do.

It was a lonesome go. I really missed Ginny. I made my rounds to other towns—Mesa, Prescott, Yuma—posting my letters for the Harts and Ginny during the off-seasons.

I felt closest to Ginny while composing letters to her by campfire. "Ginny, my love. . . My dearest Ginny. . . Ginny, darling, all I possess are cherished memories of you, my love, that linger in my marrow. . ." I penned letters of love expressing the joy and fantasies of my heart, and then closed with, "I shall carry on my trot until we are together again. I belong to you."

In Yuma, I posted my bundle of sonnets and inquired of the postmaster about the Harts. The postmaster accepted my letters but did not know of the Harts. A flurry of gunshots from outside interrupted our conversation and I left.

Down the street a cowboy was spinning around on his horse, dusting up the road, firing lead plums into the air from his six-shooter, attracting attention. "Cowboys! Cowboys! Wranglers! The Rocking $\mathcal{J}$ is hiring on hands," shouted the cowboy.

The cowboy's name was Shorty and I hired on.

When cowboying for the $\mathcal{J}$ and seeing a passing stagecoach or express wagon, I'd stop them and ask the driver to post my letters wherever they were headed, every stop along their way.

Eyeballing my letters, a driver once clutched them to his chest with jest, "Well, if you don't find Ginny, there sure are some pretty gals in Tucson."

Every day was different. You never knew what would drift by your nose. While riding out along the cliffs, scouring for mustangs, I came across a painter-artist of pictures engaged in his painting. I sat quietly watching him from my horse. He captured the feeling of the wild mustangs flying across the range and I pictured myself riding them.

The artist finished a detail with a flourish and said, "Hello."

"Howdy. You're real good with those saguaros, puffy clouds and mountains."

"Thank you."

"How long ago did those mustangs pass by?"

The artist laughed, "They're long gone, cowboy."

Before he traveled on, he sold me a small box of colors and brushes and showed me a thing or two about perspective and contrast. I learned how to mix primary colors and paint with tint, tone and shade.

During the in-betweens, I'd go off and paint a picture, trying to copy the afternoon light on the peaks or the billowing clouds floating over the range. The artist told me he was trying to capture the drama of the stormy western skies. I tried to capture the freedom of the wild mustangs galloping across the range.

Riding for the ⌡ I had my own *remuda*—a string of seven or nine horses. The *caballeros*—horsemen—always chose solid colored horses for breeding and so did I. I looked for horses with substantial breadbaskets. They could carry food for long distances, and when fording water, they swam like ducks and I'd be high and dry.

When you chose a horse, you partnered up. Cattle would charge a walking man. I never did anything alone. My life depended on whichever horse I was riding.

In all the years of cowboying, the hardest thing for me or any other cowboy was to ride his string of horses up the trail and have them sold along with the cattle on delivery.

With the herd sold and wearing three months of trail dust and stink, the outfit scrubbed up ready to let loose. We were having a soak and splashing about in a waterhole—all naked and half naked—washing our backs and our horses. Our clothes, all faded, worn out and torn, weren't worth washing.

The dry goods store would be my first stop in town.

An old gypsy wagon drove out from town and passed by our cow camp. The gentleman addressed us asking if we would like our photographs taken and our likeness recorded for posterity. Lyle told him we didn't have any photographs and asked, "Who's posterity?"

"Gentlemen, allow me to demonstrate." The photographer started explaining about photography and set up a little black box with a lens on a wood tripod. "Gentleman, please observe. This is a true remembrance—a souvenir for all time."

When I looked through the lens I could see whatever I pointed it at, but it was upside down and real small.

The photographer was a magician with grand arm-waving gestures and lingo beyond the stars. "Gentlemen, when the light passes through the lens into the camera," he paused knowing his customer, "It brands, brands an image onto a piece of glass. And hocus-pocus—it makes a picture."

Tank, one of the hands spoke up. "Mister, can you chew that hocus-pocus a little finer?"

The boys saw no real value and expressed very little interest in pictures of scenery.

The photographer surveyed the tough hides of his audience, realizing he must overcome the obstacle of buyer resistance. "Pardon me, gentlemen. I see I have failed to explain the mesmerizing power of such a photograph. For upon a gaze—a single gaze," the photographer placed his hands over his heart, closed his eyes and swooned, "Oh! Upon the gaze of a portrait of a real cowboy the ladies are predisposed to fall all over in love with the bearer of such a photograph."

I don't think the boys knew exactly what the man was talking about, but if the ladies were ready to fall in love, they were all in. They lined up.

Looking through the lens, viewing the open-air baths, the photographer was just about to snap the picture.

I glanced over and told Lyle that he might be fronting a bit too much exposure for a first impression of introductory to a faint-hearted lady. Maybe he should holster himself down into the water.

Grinning and admiring our handsomeness, it was the first time we got to see a genuine likeness of ourselves. And, at a cost of four bits each, the photographer cleaned up.

Nighthawking

I WAS NIGHTHAWKING on my favorite horse, Quincy. Gentle, surefooted and with a sense of direction, he kept one eye on the cattle and one eye on the trail. And, he could tell time. He'd stop, shake his head and drift back to camp knowing our two-hour watch was over whether I was awake or not and circle the chuck wagon until I smelled the coffee.

We had gathered and were sitting on a ⌍ herd, mostly yearlings, tallied just short of fifteen hundred head. The weather was hot, night and day, threatening to storm. The moon was on the rise and the cattle chewed their cuds, grunting and blowing over contented stomachs. I enjoyed the night motion of the moon and stars. Watching the Big Dipper, I could tell it was midnight. I had just passed my nineteenth birthday. Stargazing, I imagined Ginny looking into the glimmering heavens, gazing on the moon. I longed for my prairie madonna. Her love warmed me.

My harmonica playing was improving. It didn't scare the cattle no more. I was playing a lullaby I learned from Aiden. Nervous as cats, my playing had a way of settling 'em down for the night.

The hands were touchy over the strain of the drive, but no one was complaining. I had just gotten to sleep when Jorge, one of the guards nighthawking with me, rousted me out by bouncing pebbles off my head. Startled awake I jerked, quick-fingered, reaching for my six-shooter. It was just before daybreak. Coyotes were howling. It was my second trick at watch with him and Carver. Carver was a Negro cowboy, afraid of owls, but he near had their vision at night.

It was a foggy morning. Riding up slowly relieving grizzly Bump, one of the night guards making rounds on the herd, I found him asleep in the saddle. Bump never said much. As a matter of fact, the only time he opened his mouth was to feed it.

Riding alongside Bump, tipping and tilting in his saddle, we circled the herd twice, passing Carver and Jorge who were circling and eyeing the herd in the opposite direction. They just smiled. I tapped Bump with my quirt. Groggy, he opened his eyes, and without a word reined off back to camp.

Circling the herd, humming a tune, milling my thoughts, I became aware I was holding Ginny's pearl button in my hand, polishing it with my thumb. It glistened in the moonlight. Tallying off the years on my fingers: 1874, '75, '76, it had been three years and I still could feel her heart beat.

I had sent letters addressed general delivery, Mr. and Mrs. Virgil Hart, attention Ginny, to every town, whistle stop, military outpost and cantonment in the west.

Dozing off, barely awake, my thoughts were of Ginny. Real in my dreams, the melody of her voice played a tune in my heart. She was woven into the fabric of my imagination. Memories of Ginny flooded my head. They were all I had left. As one image drifted away, another would wash in: Ginny in sundress and bonnet in the back of the covered wagon; her reflection in the brook as it ripples and rings and the smile on her face as we were about to kiss.

Asleep in the saddle, I sang out, "Swing them pretty girls round and round." I dreamed of her dancing at the schoolhouse baile—twirling and swirling, spinning and dipping. "Ginny," I asked, "May I have this dance?"

"Oh, I'm sorry, sir my dance card is filled." And she whirled away.

And then it occurred to me, "Oh no!" I burst out. What if she has wed a finer life, forgotten me, and now plays with a parcel-load of young ones? I was startled awake.

Carver was riding alongside listening to my sleep talk. He grinned, "I'll bet your Ginny's a real peach."

"Yes, she truly is."

We circled the herd when the morning air charged up. Our horses shivered and we felt the breeze.

The day was breaking.

The Earth Quivered

THUNDER, LIGHTNING AND WIND—the earth quivered. "Smell that? Here she comes," announced Carver.

"We're gonna get wet." We pulled our hats down hard with both hands.

Black-purple storm clouds rolled in over the mountain range with the full force of Moses determined to flood hell. We tried to hold the stirring cattle on the bed ground. Lightning struck in the distance and set the desert sage grass ablaze.

"1-2-3," counted Carver. And the thunder rumbled.

The fires roared, racing across the parched mesa. The faint sound of the chuck's triangle rang out and every boot in camp was in the saddle.

Caught between the rolling clouds of thunder and lightning, the desert sky darkened. The rains poured down out of the sky with such force, the raging fires that had engulfed Skull Mesa were extinguished like breath on a candle.

Thunder clapped and the herd was up off, on the run charging Carver and Jorge, who had no choice but to swirl around and lead the stampede.

The Sun, Moon and Stars disappeared. The sky turned blacker than the inside of a mine.

The driving rain pelted down with the cutting force of a gale turning the dry, hard desert to slippery mud. We rode blind, trying to keep the cattle close in. Jamming the wind, we raced up full-out alongside the herd, trying to turn them.

In the fury, flying blind in the dark, I could only see the cattle in the flickers of lightning. The gale winds howled—the thunder rolled—and the rumble turned into one deafening drone.

Frantic, the herd blasted with pounding hooves and clacking horns towards the high cut banks and cliffs of the creek. I couldn't see my horse's head, so I gave him his, praying he could negotiate the perils of the rough terrain.

With a blinding flash and crash of thunder, a bolt of lightening struck and electrified the herd. The discharge spooled and curled flashing around their horns, sizzling and snapping, leaping from steer to steer. The herd was aglow. Their fierce, frightened eyes sparkled like emeralds. Terrified, they moved as a massive wave rising and falling—raging across the desert.

We raced lighting and thundering hooves, trying to swing the leaders and mill the herd into a round-and-round. Blind, in the mucky thick of it, running pell-mell for miles racing death, our boots filled with water. Slipping and sliding, it was all we could do to stick to our saddles. One misstep and we'd be done in.

The thunderclap 'bout made my ears bleed and the lightning saved my life. Lightning flashed and right before my eyes I watched Carver airborne with the raging herd of cattle, flailing over the edge and falling from the high bluffs plunging down into the creek.

My horse dug his forefeet into the muddy earth. With his hind feet well under him, he stopped short of the edge with such force, my face slammed into his head. Bloody and dazed, I grabbed a fistful of mane, and held on for life.

In the flashes of lightning, I saw Indians from their caves watching the river of cattle piling up in the creek. The thunder rolled on and rain sluiced down washing over the bawling, steaming cattle.

We had stayed with the herd and now there was nothing I could do. I sat in the thundering darkness, as if in church. *Dios sabe*, why wasn't I at the bottom of the pile-up? Feeling my horse's heart beating like a drum, I sat there perched on the edge. Soaking in the throbbing rain, dazed and blurry-eyed, bleeding and trembling, I embraced my gift of life.

I hadn't noticed the rain had stopped until I felt the warmth and glory of the morning rays of sunlight on my face. The cattle were still. Standing stiff in place facing the creek they sniffed the sweet breath of dawn. I called out, shattering the peaceful sounds of morning. "Jorge!"... "Carver!"... There were no answers.

My face clouded in the shadows of death. I took off my hat and said a silent prayer.

"...and may their spirits return to the Giver."

Blue Whistlers

THE WASHES RAGED, flowing with rolling muddy water, violently carrying full-grown mesquite trees away and out of sight. Huge boulders tumbled like marbles rolling past floating cattle and horses, taking out cottonwoods as if they were tinker pins in a child's game.

Sacked in their saddles, we lost two good men. Grim and silent, we buried them by the hackberry trees up in the foothills overlooking the open range. It was a grey day threatening to rain, when the funeral cortege rode up the hill leading the two horses carrying their bodies to the gravesite. The wind whistled and the rain began to drizzle.

Covered in their slickers and wrapped gently in their saddle blankets, we laid them low into their wet bunks already filling with water. We shoveled in the dirt, tamped it smooth and overlaid rocks.

A plank shelf from the chuck wagon had been cut and two headboards carved to mark the graves. Ernestro, the outfit's cook, had a flair with the blade and carved the letters real fancy.

Jorge Vásquez
Californio Vaquero
1876

I didn't know Jorge that well, but I liked him and his nature. Carver was a Sergeant in the 9th Cavalry, an all-Negro regiment, formed by the United States after the Rebellion. Dependable, self-contained—as good a horseman as I've ever shared a trail with.

On Carver's headboard, Ernestro cut:

Carver Butler
Buffalo Soldier
1876

We hung his brass bugle on the headboard.

And being all the family they had, the outfit removed their hats and silently readied for a cowboy's prayer over them. Fogged with our own feelings and thoughts, we all waited for someone to say the prayer.

With two black eyes from slamming into my horse's head, I stood there thinking, I'll not be taking tomorrow for granted.

Words did not easily rise to the occasion. Our spurs rattled lowly.

"They were my best friends! Brothers!" blurted Shorty. "Now they're with God."

"Amen!" retorted the outfit.

We fired salutes of blue whistlers from our six-shooters into the air, mounted up and silently trailed back to camp. Ernestro walked carrying the shovel.

There was work to be done.

Gloomy Company

THE STORM was like grandma's mixing bowl. Rocks, cactus, trees and limbs all whipped up every which way, frosted with mud, berries, cactus pads and sage grass, then finely decorated with the embossed tracks of quail, deer, javelina and coyote.

Turkey buzzards circled in the sky.

The cattle were scattered and many were lost. I'm sure the Indians made good use of them.

For days we all squished in our boots. We prowled for weeks rounding up horses and scouring for cattle as far as ten miles away.

I lost Ginny's pearl button in the fury of the stampede—mixed up somewhere in the sea of mud.

The storm had come and gone but the clouds of discontent lingered. Memories of Jorge and Carver played heavy on our minds. The mood of the outfit turned gloomy. Summer work was long over. With little work to keep us busy, our minds started to drift with thoughts of winter coming on.

Seven of us, what was left of the outfit, were out on the range circled up sitting on our horses, pondering our future.

"It's all I can do to put up with all your sour company," drawled Shorty, trying to lighten our mood.

"Ya won't hav' t' much longer," quipped Lyle.

"Brandin's just about wrapped up—waddies are all gone. We're next," said Cardy.

Bump sat silently listening to our wallow.

G Jakes looked around, surrounded by sad sacks. "Christmas comin' on—I got nowhere to go. Where ya' all thinkin' 'bout holin' up t' spring?"

"Tank and I was thinkin' about trying on Mexico," answered Punch.

"*Senoritas*! *Ole*!" sang Shorty, all smiles.

"I'll ride down to Mexico with you, Punch," I said, looking at the distant faces. Like me, most of the boys were rootless and strays. We didn't have families with hearth fires and warm hearts to embrace us.

The only bright cloud was seeing el Book ride into camp. He was on his way home to California to visit family for Christmas. He was looking for a hot meal and to spend the night. I was looking for a good story.

Glad the outfit had a *cocinero*—cook—el Book enjoyed Ernestro's spicy cooking and decided to stay on for awhile. What Ernestro didn't know about peppers, el Book did—compadres of the flame.

The days stayed wet and the nights turned cold. We shoveled up the mud to raise the cooking fire until the ground dried out. Wood for cooking was scarce. Ernestro, a mushroom of a man, managed his chuck peeking out from the shade of a large sombrero. He was running out of patience with the outfit and refused to make anymore cook fires by burning buffalo chips. At breakfast he shouted out the order, "There will be cold beans!—cold coffee!—cold everything, if you waddies don't gather up some wood, good dry wood, for Ernestro's fire!"

I hooked a loop around the root of a large dead cholla cactus and yanked it out of the wash.

My horse suddenly reared. Disturbed, a rattlesnake uncoiled, striking out. I drew my six-shooter, shot and holstered. As quick as that, the snake flopped dead at my horse's hooves.

I dragged the tree back to camp. About to break it up for firewood, I noticed bits of tied-off canvas and tattered colored cloth as well as brass buttons from the 9th Cavalry fastened to the branches. I bet they were Carver's. And then it struck me, this is it, the thorny, spiked sentry of the trail I had slammed into years ago, the day I was abruptly separated from Ginny. Looking over the broken tree, I had an idea.

I dug a hole between the chuck wagon and the campfire, stood the tree up and buried what was left of the gnarled root. Ernestro enjoyed pointing out WB's tree for the outfits' amusement. They laughed accusing me of trying to grow firewood.

Ernestro was a jolly sight alright, wearing a flour sack for an apron, marked XXXX. Every day upon my return to camp for meals, he religiously watered that dead cholla tree with cold coffee, teasing in broken English, "Ernestro's coffee makes WB's tree grow big and strong."

Well, the tree just stood there until Ernestro went around on the sly, gathering up green leaves and stuck them on the dead limbs. Later that night he acted surprised announcing to the outfit, "Leaves! The tree is growing leaves!"

I took a lot of ribbing around that campfire. One after another, puffin' wind, the hands were relentless. "Yes, sir, we'll be eatin' peaches from WB's orchard in the morning."

The spirit of our outfit started to grow.

It Started to Grow

AN OLD MEXICAN SPUR with silver inlay and a large rowel appeared on one of the tree limbs. A day later, a little amber glass medicine bottle hung from a branch wired up with a length of bailing-wire.

The next night, while spilling stories around the campfire, we noticed a boot stuck on the end of a branch. The flickering shadows from the fire made it look like the boot was dancing.

No one ever saw who was dressing up the tree, but it was definitely growing. From one boot, it now had four—enough for a square dance. The tree also wore a faded blue neckerchief and some horseshoes. A red jasper stone, polished by the creek, balanced between the trunk and a limb. The tree now had a heart.

And still, during all that time, none of the hands ever owned up to fooling with the tree, even though two of the old boots looked like Shorty's.

Every time I crossed paths with the tree there was another eye catcher onboard. A hand-woven black and white horse-hair lariat was looped up and down and around the branches circling the tree. Colorful river stones, white quartz, turquoise and dangling shards of hand-decorated Indian pottery adorned the branches. Fanciful attractions of brass rosettes, cobbled together with sticks, string and feathers now twisted in the wind.

As the tree grew, so did our spirits and laughter around the campfire. We accused each other of sneaking around, dressing up the tree. "Where did that huge pinecone come from?" asked Lyle. We were all pretty sure it came from Lyle.

In a matter of a few days I was afraid the tree's branches would collapse under their own weight. Canning jars, airtight peach cans with holes punched in them and shiny tin lids flashed in the sun.

Ernestro riled early one morning when he discovered the *ristra*, his string of red Mexican peppers, was missing from the chuck, taken apart and hanging like fruit all over the tree.

At breakfast he surveyed our faces, looking for the culprit or culprits who likely stole his peppers. Grinning and eyeing each other, the outfit stifled snickers.

Later that afternoon, Bump made up for our transgression of the peppers when he presented a delighted Ernestro with his cowboy hat filled with hen fruit, speckled wild turkey eggs, for Christmas breakfast.

Out of the Darkness

CHRISTMAS EVE was upon us. The Moon hung bright in the western sky, placed there by the hand of God, as an ornament in the fields of twinkling stars decorating the earth.

The horses and kitchen mules shivered and shook in the crisp desert night air, extending their heads over the makeshift corral to watch the commotion.

We gathered around our Christmas tree sharing cheer, good will and the warmth of the fire. I cut a candle into pieces and placed them into the canning jars and peach cans. They glowed real pretty.

There was cowboy bragging with old tales that may have once had a speck of truth to them, but through years of retelling had soared with imagination to full-out fancy.

Lyle's laughing, he's crying in the middle of telling a windy story. "So Tank and me's with this new outfit on a drive north out of Texas. Tank's nighthawkin', asleep in the saddle, circlin' the herd.

No one bothers to wake him, and his hoss goes to roundin' up strays.

All night long his hoss does the work fo' both of 'em, headin' off and retrievin' cows. Come mornin' when the rest of the hands ride up ready to drive the herd, here's Tank circlin'—still asleep. But now there are about twenty, thirty buffalo bedded down, enjoyin' the good company of the herd."

Tank protested, "Now there you go again stretching the wire, Lyle. There was only nine or ten of them buffaloes."

Lyle shrugged, "So then the boys in the outfit wanted to know where we learned to punch cattle and if mama had any more boys at home like us."

"That's some windy tale, Lyle. You're startin' to collect flies."

"That's the Texas truth!" roared Lyle.

"That's when cows climb trees," popped Cardy.

Shined boots and buckles, clean shirts and smiles, we toasted and clinked our cups. Merriment all around until the mules brayed, the horses riled and the trail dog barked, sensing a presence off in the darkness.

Tank reached for a rifle, and shouted, "Who's out there?" Cocking his Winchester, "Show yourselves!"

A stranger's voice answered out, "Hold on. I'm alone. I'm coming in." Riding slowly out of the darkness of the cold desert night into the firelight, a stranger on a steaming horse appeared. And, to our surprise, he was followed by three snorting, steaming wild mustangs.

Wearing a serape, he was a striking cowboy with a mustache over a smile and chin beard. He had an easy way. Reining up and dismounting his lathered horse, he said, "These mustangs wear no brand. Found 'em on the range. Figured they might be yours."

Tank replied, "No, they ain't ours, stranger," disengaging the hammer and lowering his rifle.

With a gesture of his hand, the stranger said, "Then, consider 'em my gift. I'm traveling light tonight."

Well, we were all pretty amazed. I never saw wild mustangs follow anything but the sun and their own shadows. And I'm sure neither did el Book or any of the wranglers.

Looking around, the stranger said, "It's been a long ride. And the wind blows cold. Be alright with you, fellas, if I share your fire awhile?"

Tank nodded, observing the horses. "Join us. You've been traveling fast. Racin' the devil are ya'?"

As the stranger answered, he began to strip the gear off his horse and grinned, "I'm working on it." The three wild mustangs stood by pawing dirt.

"Where y'all goin' in such a hurry?" Tank inquired. "These hosses are spent."

Bump interrupted, speaking up, amazing us all, "Feed and water's over here, partner."

"Well now, ain't Bump overflowing with words," quipped Punch.

"Much obliged." The stranger motioned, "Git." His horse moved off with Bump and the three mustangs followed along. Turning back to Tank, he answered, "I'm riding to town to celebrate my birth."

Ernestro walked up grinning hospitality and handed the stranger a cup of cheer. "Happy Birthday, *amigo*. And, *Feliz Navidad*. This'll warm you up."

The stranger smiled with appreciation, *"Feliz Navidad."* Looking at me and the rest of the hands gathered around, "Thank you all for your fire."

Celebrating the spirit of Christmas, the stranger joined our circle of stories, tales and show. G-Jakes, good with rope tricks, skipped in and out of a loop twirling it from side to side, showing off his stuff.

The stranger listened and laughed as el Book spun a funny story about a coyote, a mule and the frog.

Ernestro poured wine from a jug into 'cowboy crystal'—canning jars he had saved for the occasion. Shorty passed the jars around. Ernestro raised his glass and proposed a toast, "Feliz Navidad." Raising our jars, we returned the toast, "Feliz Navidad."

It was Ernestro's night to shine and he was ready. Missing a finger, he had a reputation for his one-finger chili. Tonight we would feast on his chili verde and corn tamales, both holiday favorites. A wagon plank was rigged to the chuck wagon and set up with bowls and baskets of mesquite-smoked corn bread.

Bump was winning at a fast game of checkers. Punch pondered, planning his next move. "King me."

It was a dandy party, jolly all around sharing the holiday spirit.

Ernestro removed the Dutch ovens from the coals. Striking the chuck's triangle, he announced, "Chili time!"

As the night unfolded, the stranger trailed into a story, a word, something to say to each one of us. Laughing with enthusiasm, he told his own bronc-busting story. "Screwed on tight, I was ready. The roan left the ground pawin' at the moon. He was flyin' so crooked all I could see were the birds in the sky. He was so high you could see mountain peaks and tree tops 'neath him. And then we parted company. He sailed me through the air and I fell from the clouds bustin' the earth."

I was gazing on the moon when the stranger wandered over and saw the harmonica in my pocket. "You any good with that harp?"

"The cattle like it."

He smiled, "May I?" I handed it over. Tapping it on his hand, he paused, "You know, riding in tonight, I spotted a number of mustangs and wild cattle up in the hills along the ridges, bushed up, hidden in the mesquites and roughs. Good pickin's for a brush popper."

"A storm came through awhile ago and really scattered 'em." Studying the stranger, he struck me familiar and I asked, "Have we met before?"

"Maybe so. I've been a lot of places. Ever been to Santa Fe?"

"No, sir. Is that where you got your hat?"

The stranger smiled proudly, shaping the broad brim. "Nice one, isn't it?"

"It fits you fine," I said. "Best I've seen.

Mouthing the harmonica, he said, "This is a favorite of mine." He began to play.

"I never heard that one. What's it called?"

"*The Cowboy's Lament*."

"I like it."

Draining the last of the wine into a jar, Ernestro slammed down the empty wine jug and loudly announced, "We's out of wine!"

We laughed, "Out of wine? What? You just don't

know how to pour a jug." The stranger glanced over at the jug, laughing, enjoying the moment.

Ernestro snapped back in good humor, "I know how to work a jug." He jerked it up over his head to show the jug was empty. Wine gushed out, splashing him. We all roared with laughter. The merriment around the fire and our Christmas tree continued as we enjoyed our meal and each other's company.

Boomer, the trail dog, jumped in and out of a spinning loop for treats. Bits and pieces of cowboy yarns and tales peppered the night. "Remember Pack Rat's raucous runaway mules breakin' free from the wagon? They's draggin' their rings 'n trace chains; rattlin' 'n skiddin' over them flint rocks—sparkin' 'n blazin' up trails of fire!"

Over by the fire, the stranger put the cover back on the Dutch oven. He and Ernestro were engaged in spirited conversation in Spanish, with animated gestures of chopping, stirring and rolling like two cooks sharing recipes and secrets. The stranger must have liked the chili verde. Offering payment, he put two canning jars of it in his saddlebags. Ernestro waved him off. The stranger insisted and Ernestro relented, cheerfully wrapping up some of the mesquite-smoked cornbread as well.

The spirit and bonds of fellowship shined as the candles on the tree glowed. I pulled out my harmonica and began playing the only Christmas song I knew, *Silent Night*. One by one, the cowboys removed their hats. The glow on the Christmas tree and on their faces, standing around as I played, was a sight for poor eyes.

The flames of the campfire slowly cooled and burned down to glowing embers.

Thanks for Your Song

EARLY CHRISTMAS MORNING, awakened by the lingering smell of smoke and coffee on the coals, we heard Ernestro's jolly voice, "Shine and arise, waddies. *Feliz Navidad.* Give the glory to God."

We slowly wandered up to the breakfast fire. Ernestro was cracking turkey eggs into a skillet when he glanced up at the Christmas tree. *"Gloria a Dios!"* he whispered to himself. Rising up and not believing his eyes, he stumbled backwards.

The golden rays of the morning sun highlighted the now much-alive cholla, abloom with red blossoms and yellow fruit hanging from the barbed ocher branches. Cactus wrens chirped and flittered about the blossoms.

In awe and wonder, we slowly approached our Christmas tree. Struck by a ray of sunlight, the stranger's cowboy hat hung on a branch. I carefully removed it from the tree. Inside the hat was a note. I read it aloud to the camp, "WB, thank you for your song. You'll find Ginny in Santa Fe. —Sunny. Merry Christmas. God bless you all."

Well, we all stood there, looking at the tree and looking at each other in amazement. I put on the cowboy hat. It was a good fit.

Hungry, I stayed just long enough to finish breakfast.

Asking around about the trails to Santa Fe, el Book had more than the answer. "Fly to your darling *querida.*" And with a flair for romance, he told me, "You will want to ride the old Spanish trail from California that crosses the Arizona Territory to New Mexico, and then to the town of romance, *La Villa Real de la Santa Fe de San Francisco de Assisi.*" It rolled off his tongue like a song. And with a big smile, "Called 'Santa Fe' by the Americano." And he went on to say, "*La Villa* was built in 1611 when Spain owned all the known land to the north and west of the Mississippi River to the Pacific Ocean."

Ready, Button?

NEW MEXICO figured to be a long ride. I picked up my lariat and saddle. Looking over the horses in the camp's corral, the mustangs Sunny gifted the outfit took my eye. Three year olds, they were probably just shedding the last of their colt teeth. I especially liked the grulla mustang, grey with shades of purple. He was big for a mustang. My guess was he's fifteen hands.

The cowboys made their way to the rail. Topping off a bronc always made for a good show. Thinking this ought to be fun, they weren't betting on WB.

We cut the other horses from the corral. Having busted my share of rough strings, this mustang appeared to be more horse than any bronc I'd ever broke. I built a fast loop as I entered the corral. The mustang circled around, sizing me up out of the corner of his eye. He's probably thinking, 'this won't take long, button.'

I tried to look fearless while thinking about taking an ear, getting him down and tying foot-ropes. With him down, I could lace up my saddle, slide on and ride him up.

The hands were all worked up, looking for a good time.

Sparring with me, the mustang stopped. Working his ears, he swung his head and circled me in the opposite direction, challenging my courage. Cocking the rope, I let the loop fly. The rope hissed singing as it left my hand. I was ready to dally the rope around the snubbing post. But the loop flopped and the boys went wild.

Reloading, I gathered up the rope and shook out a quick loop. The mustang snorted, reversed his direction and raced around the corral. But before I could throw again, he cut up the center and abruptly hit a dead stop.

I got the feeling our introduction was over.

Looking over this powerful mustang and then over to the hands, they were as surprised as I was.

Punch handed me the blanket. I slowly approached the mustang. All hands were quiet on the rail. That mustang glanced over at me and my folly and tipped me a wink. Yes he did. I placed the blanket on his back without him flinching or raising hair.

Not a peep from the boys. I don't think they wanted to jinx me.

Punch handed me the saddle and slowly backed away. Taking a deep breath, I eased the wood onto his back. Reaching under for the cinch, "I'll just get this out of the way and we'll get this fandango on..." The stallion quivered and whisked my face with his tail. I jumped back. But, again the stallion stood firm and let me lace up the cinch. I laced it real tight.

No two horses are ever the same, but this mustang was just plain smart. Holding the reins, I talked softly slowly slipping the bosal over his nose.

I was so thrown off my game, that at best I'd be a champion or the clown. Time would tell.

With the reins in my left hand, I eased my foot into the stirrup, and grabbed a hold of his mane. The mustang shuttered and shook, unnerving me. I jerked back, "First I get on, then we play." I swung aboard quickly taking a fast set. Nothing happened. "It's time to have fun." He just stood there motionless.

The outfit held their breath.

"Maybe he's sleeping, show 'em your boot hooks!" yelled Tank. Hootin' and hollerin', the boys rallied.

With shouts and whistles, "Merry Christmas. Ya' got a merry-go-round the posies under ya'."

As I sat on that stone monument, I felt foolish, but held firm knowing he had it in him. The mustang slowly turned his head and caught my eye with a look I'll not forget. One of the wranglers yelled, "Surprise horse. You got company aboard."

Well, that bronc flattened his ears and his nostrils flared. He swung around, hung his head, arched his back, and ignited like dynamite. He tried to fly! We left the earth like blasted rock. I fanned him with my hat and kept fanning him on every jump. He landed crooked and so hard my teeth rattled and my eyes rolled.

High and wide, jump after jump, we gained air and got to spinning in circles. Whipping up the dirt into a storm of dust, the hootin' cowboys disappeared and in the center of the blinding storm, so did my shadow. I pulled up my neckerchief and closed my eyes. I was alone in the silence of myself. Swirling around on the back of this mustang spinner took everything I had. Reaching down deep, I discovered strength I had before only imagined.

With wild stiff-legged plunges, I thumbed him in the shoulders and stayed back in the wood. He landed hard, time after time, popping me in the saddle. When the dust cleared the boys cheered, surprised I was still aboard.

The mustang wheeled and bucked and scattered the hooting outfit off the corral ropes and dusted them onto the seats of their pants.

It felt like he was breaking in two. His head went one way and his hind end the other. Ernestro smiled the biggest smile and yelled, "*Viva! Magnifico! Viva!*"

Thinking he settled out, this sunfisher would go off again. Bucking, jumping and twisting, he tried to flip me into the sun. He was tiring and so was I. How much more could I take? How much more could this honest pitcher deliver? A lot!

At the top of his flight, I felt it coming. With explosive energy, this high roller whirled and flipped over backwards, popping me free and clear. Falling, I watched the powerful horse tumble and bounce in a storm of dust. I rolled and landed solid right beside him straight up in my boots. "*Viva!*" cheered el Book. "*Viva!*"

Dazed, wild-eyed and snorting, the mustang recovered, shaking it off. Thrashing to his feet, I stepped aboard and rode him up. The outfit went off hooting and howling with ear-splitting whistles.

What this pioneer bucker hadn't reckoned on was a cowboy in love was not to be thrown off his course. I stayed steady and stuck tight in the saddle.

He whipped his head around—yes he did. He reached around, grabbed my chap with his teeth and tried to pull me off. I hit him with my Christmas present. Boy, I hated to crease Sunny's Stetson. And, just when I felt myself slipping off, he turned good, broke into a rough trot and smoothed out.

Yipping, hollering and fanning their hats, the boys went wild. "*Mas! Mas! Mas!*" shouted Ernestro.

The mustang began a parade trot with his head held high and ears straight up. Getting comfortable in the saddle, I got the feeling he was satisfied that I had qualified to enjoy the privilege of riding upon his back.

Circling the corral in a smooth trot, I smiled, looking at my shadow, realizing I had chosen well.

Ernestro packed provisions. I wished everyone 'Merry Christmas,' and said goodbye to my pards, who were all teasing, 'lover boy.'

"Merry Christmas, lover boy."

"There goes another one."

"He'll soon be roofed in, clerkin' in town at the dry goods store."

"Kiss her for me."

"Kiss your darling *querida* for all of us."

"*Feliz Navidad!*"

Wild Rush

AFTER THE CIRCUS ride I just experienced, the trail to Santa Fe was a breeze.

Storm was quite a horse. Crouched low on his back, I imagined the riders of the Pony Express.

Storm leaped to a gallop.

Blazing across the open range, I had plenty to be thankful for.

With the mustang's powerful strides, his nostrils flared and the musical beat of long, loping hooves pounded out a rhythm on the skin of the earth. My thoughts wandered over the moments I had encountered crisscrossing the far West searching for Ginny. I had experienced the awesome beauty of a land far more beautiful and bigger than any dream. And to be a part, even a small part, of something so grand humbles you in its presence and embraces your spirit.

Wild and free, I was alive.

In what appeared to have happened in a breath and a heartbeat, I had experienced love and sorrow, and moments with lasting memories.

The thrill of it all!

The fruits of pain; the laughter of Indians; the motion of the moon and stars; stories of the caballeros; the faces and ways of vaqueros and cowboys I trailed and shared chuck with; the gold in sunsets and pards I had seen for the last time.

Being there was a gift.

I was alive and thankful for the smell of mesquite campfires and morning coffee when the sun first blinks; for the way the desert is perfumed with the fragrance of creosote after thunderstorms; and every day, for the drama the light creates in the skies and on the mountains, canyons, rivers, and ranges.

Sunny was right about cowboying. I had found my way. And when I'm over and laid under, I'll be ready to cross over—now that I've ridden in paradise.

Galloping full out, riding in harmony on a free spirit across the plains, I looked up at the red-tailed hawks riding the thermals in the clear sky high above me.

Glancing at my shadow with my arms stretched out like wings, I felt the wild rush.

I was flying.

Aboard this powerful horse, standing in the stirrups, raised off the saddle, leaning into the wind I crowed, "I AM A COWBOY! *Gloria a Dios!*"

Ginny was just over the horizon.

Shined Real Pretty

SANTA FE was in a green valley surrounded by blue mountains. A beautiful Spanish town of flat roofed adobe shops and houses built around a central plaza, shaded by cottonwoods.

Riding in, I passed traders and tourists, men wearing serapes, and Indian women wearing colorful woven cloth effortlessly carrying baskets on their heads filled with fruit and grain.

I made my way to the general store, which also served as the post office. I inquired about my letter of general delivery I had posted three months ago. I was surprised the clerk recalled it so quickly, "Yes, the letter was picked up just before Christmas. Nice folks, the Harts. New to the territory."

"Was their daughter with them?"

"No, sir. Just him and the missus."

My heart sunk and my face flushed. Shaken, my pale mood must have been obvious.

"Are you alright, sir?"

"Did they mention their whereabouts?"

"They didn't. You may want to inquire at Meade's Mercantile & Supply. Mr. Hart said something about digging a water well."

Just about to leave, I asked him if there was a watchmaker or jeweler in town. The clerk pointed towards Meade's. "Van Haren's. Samuel may be able to cater to your fancy. It's on your way."

"Thank you, sir."

Van Haren's shop showcased some very fine watches. Over in the corner, some cowboys were shuffling about anxiously eyeing a fancy wooden clock hung on the wall. Approaching the clerk I asked, "What's all the commotion about?"

The clerk replied, "Oh, they're waitin' on the bird to step out."

"When will that happen?"

"On the hour—every hour."

The door to the shop opened and another cowboy scooted in and over to the clock. "Did I miss it?"

Turning back to the clerk I said, "It must be quite a performance."

"Since those boys come to town, they've been in here every day just before noon to hear it tweet. Now, what can I do for you, sir?"

I told the jeweler just what I wanted and he said he could have it crafted. His eyes popped when I plopped the gold nugget down on the counter. "This ought to cover it. Make it out of this, and the rest is for you."

The clerk beamed and his, "Thank y..." was interrupted by, "Cuckoo! Cuckoo!" The bird flapped its wings, "Cuckoo!" And opened its beak with every, "Cuckoo!" The cowboys went wild with chorus— whistling, clucking, spinning around and laughing. "Cuckoo!" I'd never seen anything like it.

Turning back to the smiling clerk, he repeated,

"Thank you again, sir. This is more than generous."

Loaded with information, I took the wagon road north to Taos—a road of breathtaking views and vivid color where homesteads with barbwire, were cropping up and beginning to crowd the open range.

After a while, I spotted a pile of lumber and pipe and a man walking about a property with an adobe home, outbuildings and corrals. Riding up, I recognized Virgil with his Arkansas toothpick strapped to his side.

He surprised me when he spoke first. "Walker Brady! Look at you, boy. You've grown up."

Blushing, I stepped down and said, "Howdy, Mr. Hart. Good to see you." We shook hands.

"Good to see you, Walker. That's quite a horse you have there."

"He's something alright. What'cha doin'?"

"Lookin' for water," said Virgil. With something on his mind and getting right to it, he said, "I've been expecting you."

"You received my post?"

"Oh, I've been expecting you before that."

"What do you mean?"

"Ginny's been running off looking for you."

I got back on Storm anxious to get going. "How long has she been gone?"

"Hold on there! Wait. Let me explain. . . C'mon down. . . Ma and I had to chase after Ginny more than once to fetch her back home."

"Really?"

"Yes," Virgil answered. "Can you imagine a lonesome dove like Ginny wandering about in Dodge City?"

Taken aback, I answered, "Yes, sir, I can. That would not be good."

Nodding in agreement, Mr. Hart watched me with a serious eye. "Ginny's fine."

We stood around kicking the dirt and talked for a while, catching up. Virgil thanked me for my letter and I told him I had scoured the west looking for Ginny.

Off in the distance a ranch wagon was racing, dusting up the road. I told Virgil of my days mining for gold and growing up cowboying.

Watching the wagon get closer, "Neighbors," said Virgil. "We never did stop at the gold fields."

"What about Wickenburg?"

"Not there either. The Vulture Mine was booming, but you had to contend with the Apaches, they controlled the land."

"No wonder I couldn't find you."

Looking out at the galloping team, the wagon was drawing closer, 'Neighbors' nothing! It was too far for me to make out her features, but I recognized the whistle. Ginny was snapping the reins and racing like she was delivering the mail!

My heart raced. Virgil and I watched as she rolled up the drive. Ginny stopped the team and sat there in the wagon just staring at us. My hands got sweaty and my smile got toothy. Ginny was just as pretty as ever.

Without saying a word, she climbed down off the wagon. She started walking, then running and by the time she reached me, she was charging with the running power of a deer.

Smiling almost to tears, "WB!" Ginny launched

herself into my arms.

I spun her around to keep us both from falling.

Hugging her tightly, our hearts beat as one. "You found me. Where have you been?"

"Looking for you, darling." With Ginny's arms around me, we were alone and lost in each other's embrace. We hugged. We kissed—our hearts were on fire igniting our passion.

Virgil, all smiles for the first time, raised his finger about to speak and then paused, "I'll go tell Mrs. Hart you're here. She'll be very happy to see you."

With tears in our eyes, Ginny and I drifted off in love and caught up right where we left off.

Standing under the ramada as the sun set, Mrs. Hart called for us, "Ginny, Walker, supper."

At supper we celebrated our reunion. I played a song on the harmonica. All smiles, Pa liked my music.

Ginny had an announcement, "Mother, Father. . . W and I are in love. . ."

Virgil sprang up so quickly, his chair fell over and he surprised me with a heartfelt hug, "Welcome to the family, son." And then, hugs all around.

It was good to be with family. Virgil was truly happy I had returned and that his vigil was over. He and Mrs. Hart could finally rest easy.

The next morning, Virgil and I were up early walking about looking for water. "Shallow or deep?" I asked.

"What's the difference?"

"If it's shallow, we'll just chase down the horny toads. They own all the surface water."

"And for a well?"

"For a well, we'll have to dowse."

I cut a fresh branch for a dowsing stick from a mesquite tree and we dowsed for water.

We familied for the next few weeks: working, laughing, planning our wedding, digging a well, raising a windmill, and sharing good times.

Ginny chose to be married in the *San Francisco de Assisi Church, Ranchos de Taos.* The priest, in jest, took pride in telling us, "The Franciscan Fathers started construction in 1772 and finished quickly, 43 years later in 1815." The Church was the most beautiful building I'd ever been in.

The sight of Ginny in the glow of the altar candles took my breath away. She was beautiful, wearing flowers in her hair. She and her mother each wore a Spanish *rebozo*—fine silk-striped shawls, Ginny's was white. I was beaming. Mama was all tears. Pa was all smiles.

Ginny's gold wedding ring shined real pretty. I held her hand and the priest began, "Together your love will share the blessings of life. . ."

With our vows and in the moment of, 'I do,' we began forever together.

I surprised Pa and gave him a pocket watch after the ceremony. Mama wanted a portrait of the family. As the photographer was setting up his black camera box on a tripod, I asked the priest for a candle.

Hand in hand, Ginny and I held the burning candle together with Mama and Pa at our sides. And with a flash in the pan, we had our matrimonial family portraiture recorded for posterity.

"Merry Christmas, Cowboy"

AFTER THE WEDDING, Ginny and I headed back to Arizona in a trail wagon pulled by a team of army mules her parents gave us for a wedding present.

Wandering a new trail, we honeymooned and took our time drifting southwest. The fragrance of spring was in the air. The chuparosa along the washes and the brittlebush were blooming everywhere. The ends of the coachwhip branches of the ocotillo were covered with bright red flowers.

Storm trotted along. He still had his spirit. I never tied, tethered or hobbled him. He was free to roam at any time. Ginny was managing the team. I was playing her a new tune. I could tell she was impressed.

The trail looked so different coming from the other direction. Nothing seemed familiar. We stopped the wagon and Ginny tied off the team. We stood up and gazed over the horizon. "Sure is a big sky."

"Yes it is. And, it's all ours." We hugged and kissed.

Standing there in God's country, Ginny noticed something. "What's that?"

Narrowing my eyes, they roved the distant hills. "What's what?" I couldn't hang my eyes on it, "What am I looking for?"

Ginny pointed, "Over there, a glint of light, a speck on the horizon. It comes and goes. You drive and I'll keep an eye out for it."

"Git up." I snapped the reins and we left the wagon road weaving our way across the range. I didn't know where we were going but we were on our way.

The sun was high in the sky by the time I got a glimpse of what Ginny had seen miles back. Off in the distance, below the foothills of the Seven Sisters Mountains on the horizon, was a bright shimmering light. "See it?" Ginny pointed.

"I do now. It'll be near sunset by the time we get there."

"What do you think it is?" said Ginny.

Snapping the reins, "Git! We'll find out."

As we moved along, chasing the shimmering light, I remembered Sunny's words and kept an eye out for cattle on the ridges of the high country. Watching Storm, I was pretty sure there were wild mustangs around.

Off in the distance, the mountains reflected twilight tints of violet against a gold magenta sky.

Our shadows were long and violet and the sun was three fingers off the horizon when we arrived. The shining light had disappeared miles back.

We were approaching the spot where Ginny thought the shimmering light had first appeared. As we rode up, off in the shade, I noticed a Dutch oven hanging on a hook from a steel tripod. Ernestro's?

Imagine that.

Looking around, I searched for other remnants and traces of our cow camp, there were none. And before I could stop the wagon, Ginny called out, "This is it! Whoa!"

I reined up the mules. "This is what?"

"Where we're going to live—our homestead." Ginny jumped down from the wagon. "Over there." Now running to 'over there', she exclaimed, "This is where we'll build our home. Where we'll raise our family."

I just sat there in the wagon smiling, watching her run about. Ginny was so excited.

"Right here, we'll build our home right here. I'll put my garden over there."

I pulled out my harmonica and put music to her dance.

Ginny skipped and swirled around excitedly in rhythm with the land, plotting and planning. "Where shall we put our chicken coop?" she asked.

I looked around, and thought out loud, "This would be a good place to call home." Jumping off the wagon, I was pretty worked up myself. "Whoa!" The chain fruit cholla Christmas tree caught my eye and stopped me in my tracks.

As I walked over to the Christmas tree, I could hear the excitement in Ginny's voice, "And we'll hang a swing on the cottonwood tree. We can wash our clothes in the creek. . ."

Abloom with blossoms, cactus wrens had made their nest with ribbons of grass in one of the branches.

A rolled up piece of paper with a string around it was stuffed into one of the cowboy boots. Pulling it out, I unwound the string. The message took me by surprise and made me smile. I rolled up the paper and stuffed it back into the boot.

Ginny joined me and took my hand. "Your Christmas tree, it's beautiful." Admiring the tree's trimmings, Ginny removed her bracelet and slipped it onto a branch.

Gazing at Ginny, "And so are you, darlin'."

A glimmer from the tree caught Ginny's eye. "Oh my!" she beamed with surprise, "Where did you ever find it?" reaching out to touch and spin the button.

Sure enough to my amazement, hanging there from a thread, was Ginny's pearl button aglow in the sun.

Imagine that. . . .

I smiled—we kissed. Embraced in each other's arms, Ginny whispered, "Merry Christmas, cowboy."

The amber bottle and jars sparkled with the sun backlighting the shimmering branches of golden thorns.

The excitement of our future together carried on as the sun set.

The Dutch oven was on the coals.

In the warm glow of the campfire, our hearts celebrated. Our Christmas tree glowed pretty with candles in the night. Forever in love, we watched the crackling flames of the fire as sparks drifted up into the desert sky to mingle with the twinkling stars.

The Moon hung bright in the western sky.

★   ★   ★   ★   ★

ABOUT THE AUTHOR

TOM VAN DYKE lives with Mary, his wife, on their ranch in Cave Creek, Arizona. A member of Western Writers of America, he has been writing screenplays since 1970. One of his motion pictures was considered for nomination of an Academy Award ®.

Tom created and wrote the American Bicentennial television public service announcements, *Stand Up and Be Counted*, the most widely viewed national and international PSAs in the history of television.

His creative expression of writing and film production is shared with his creation of fine art. Tom's sculptures, paintings and photography have been exhibited or are in the permanent collections of the NY Museum of Modern Art, the Carnegie Art Institute, the Buffalo Bill Historical Center, the Detroit Institute of Arts, the Henry Ford Museum, the Cranbrook Institute of Arts, and the Butler Institute of American Art.

A Cowboy Christmas An American Tale is Tom's first book.

Visit: ACowboyChristmas.com

for Special Features and Particulars.